THE MASKS WE WEAR

NOT ALL RELATIONSHIPS LAST FOREVER

RODNEY LAMARR

Edited by
Mir-Yashar Seyedbagheri

TRIGGER WARNING

This work of fiction contains sensitive events and topics. Please be aware that the following triggers are present in the book:

- Underage drinking
- Sexual assault
- Bullying
- Racism
- Violence towards juveniles
- Explicit language

While I want to engage in thoughtful conversations surrounding difficult themes, the well-being of readers is my priority. I appreciate your interest in reading my work, but remember that your well-being matters.

THE MASKS WE WEAR

NOT ALL RELATIONSHIPS LAST FOREVER

RODNEY LAMARR

Edited by
Mir-Yashar Seyedbagheri

TABLE OF CONTENTS

TABLE OF CONTENTS

CHAPTER ONE

EMMA

"My name is Emma Mai Thomas."

The earth seemed uneasy as the moon peeked from the smoky cover, revealing an unfamiliar world. There were no animals, no birds. Even the bugs seemed to have vanished. I turned back but could only see the stillness of the forest, blanketed in a cloud of smoke. My breathing grew frantic as I stopped and waited. Twisted shadows flickered through the darkness, creating imaginary foes. I turned and ran.

"My name is Emma Mai Thomas. I live at 409 Chestnut Street."

My heart raced as I jumped over fallen trees. Branches reached for me, ripping skin from flesh as I dodged through the night. My feet pounded against the ground, snapping twigs and branches. Rocks and stones kissed the soles of my feet as I cut through the awakened trees. Voices cried out.

"My name is Emma Mai Thomas. I live at 409 Chestnut Street. I am eight years old."

The vast darkness grew still, broken only by the falling embers of fire. The air was thick with smoke as trees cried out in pain. I could taste my blood flowing through my veins. My heart pounded like a drum, beating to my every thought.

"My name is..."

CHAPTER TWO
EMMA
Nine years later

My body shot up as Ariana Grande's "7 Rings" blasted from my cell phone. I glanced around the room, trying to get my bearings. I fumbled for my phone, canceling the alarm. Leaning back down, I stared at the ceiling and took a few deep breaths.

Rays of sunlight trickled through the window, casting light into the still room. The silence inside was muted by the birds chirping outside. After a few moments, I slumped over to the bathroom.

The hot water bit against my skin as I lowered my head, watching the water pour off my body. The air grew heavy as steam floated into existence.

After my shower, I stared in the mirror, running the brush through my tangled hair. The crunching echoed in the room while water sprinkled against the mirror.

"You got this. It's just another day. Another day at school," I said, staring at the mirror. Even my reflection had little faith that those words were true. But still, I finished getting dressed.

When I walked into the kitchen, the smell of burnt coffee lingered in the air. Bread crumbs rested on the counter next to an empty sliced cheese wrapper. The subtle hint of Irish Spring faded out of existence. Dad must have just left for work.

I looked at the dim scene. An eerie silence crept over the room. Dishes piled in the sink, stained pots and pans dwelled on the stove, and the tapping of water splashing against an overflowing pot rang throughout the room.

On the table, the remains of once-fresh sunflowers sat in the middle, begging for the smallest amount of water. Its withered stem leaned as its pedals faded, almost looking transparent. A small yellow sticky note clung to the counter. It read:

"Going to the cemetery this weekend. You should come. Love, Dad."

I cringed at the idea of going. I had never liked cemeteries, and my parents knew that. Something about walking over a dead person just to relive memories with another dead person didn't make sense to me. Shaking my head, I poured the remaining coffee into a used mug, but there wasn't enough for a full cup.

"Dang it," I muttered.

The bitterness of the cold coffee splashed against my tongue, instantly scrunching my face. I shook my head and set the mug in front of the decayed flowers. My mind couldn't help but retrace what this place used to be.

My memory slowly took shape as a younger me walked into the kitchen after a nice warm shower. Grease clouded the room as bacon popped from the skillet. Mom greeted me with her sweet smile and slid a full plate in my direction: fresh, pillow-like eggs, three strips of almost burnt bacon, and a piece of buttered sourdough toast.

"So, what were you saying about a party?" She slid another plate for Dad onto the table and returned to the kitchen. "I didn't think you were a party person," she said in the kitchen entryway.

"I'm totally not," I said, breaking apart a slice of bacon. Small bits fell to my plate, landing in my eggs. Michael wants me to go, so…"

"Michael, huh?"

Her eyebrows rose, and I could feel the heat of her stare.

"We're just friends," I said, rolling my eyes.

"Mmhmm. When I was your age girls didn't hang out with boys as much as you and Michael do, unless marriage was in the cards."

"Sure, Mom." I shook my head.

"Babe?"

Dad stomped in, interrupting our conversation. His muscular figure filled the doorframe. His hair still dripped from his shower, soaking his freshly ironed shirt.

"Babe, where did I put my..." he asked, but before he could finish, Mom was already ready with a response.

"On the couch, hun."

It was always like that. Their connection was so deep that she would finish his sentences. Either that, or he was just predictable. Yeah, he was probably just predictable.

He peeked over the couch, and sure enough, there they were. His keys were tucked between the cushions, a sign that he fell asleep in his work clothes while watching the latest police detective shows. He wrapped his arms around her tiny frame to show appreciation, snuggling her neck. This filled the house with giggles and "Oh stop, I'm cooking," as she disappeared into his arms.

The warmth of it all brought a smile to me. But my smile soon dissipated, as if it were just a memory. The brightness of the past soon faded, and my dull present took form once again.

"Mom," I shouted. After a few seconds, I yelled again but received the same response. Only the stillness of the house replied. She never went to work this early. I sighed. I would have loved for at least one of my parents to stay home from work, if just to wish me good luck on my first day back. Yep, if this was any indication of how this day was going to go, then I was doomed.

CHAPTER THREE
MICHAEL

"Michael, wake up. You have like ten minutes, and I can't take you to school today!"

I pulled the covers from my head and peered at my mom in the doorway. Her eyes flicked from me to the ceiling as she tilted her head, trying to insert her earrings.

"I'm up. I'm up," I said, my voice hoarser than usual.

"And you forgot to do the dishes last night."

"Sorry," I mumbled.

"Always sorry," she said. "You need to…"

I quickly grabbed my earbuds from the nightstand and popped them in, drowning her annoying voice under the bass of blink-182's "Adam's Song."

A gigantic yawn stretched across my face as I kicked my legs over the bed. With a few rocks, I was on my feet, dragging myself to the bathroom. There was no time for a shower, so I opted for a few splashes of cold water and a slight mist of body spray.

Next, I swished a cup full of mouthwash, letting the chemicals burn the horrible breath away. Then, I opened my mouth, revealing shining teeth. I rubbed my finger across, slightly rotating my head to get a better angle.

After a few strokes of my brush through my hair, I was good to go. I grabbed my backpack and headed down to the kitchen.

When I passed Mom's room, I peered inside. She paced back and forth, stepping over clothes tossed to the floor. Behind her was a large half-made bed. You could tell which side was hers because the sheets were tossed about.

Even though Dad had been gone for years— four years, eight months, and three weeks to be exact—she still refused to sleep on his side, or at least in the middle. Dad died in a "freak accident" due to a mechanical mishap in the engine room while deployed onboard the USS Vicksburg. All thanks to a pipe bursting, causing the engine room to flood. He managed to save his crew but couldn't get himself out in time. A stupid and avoidable accident that ruined both of us, and honestly, neither one of us had been the same.

"Mr. Marshall, I've been at this company for four years….no, no. Mr. Marshall, I have been a dedicated employee for...crap," she said, raising her balled fist.

Dad's death had taken its toll on her. I remembered when she used to smile, every inch of her face contorted itself to express her joy. That smile healed my broken bones when I first fell off my bike. It filled my heart when I recited my favorite knock-knock jokes as a kid. It was that smile that mended me when bullies tried to rip me down. But now, her smiles were replaced by endless scowls and so much hate and pain I feared it had swallowed her whole.

She just isn't the same anymore, not at work, not at home, not with me. Heck, she can barely stand the sight of me now. She used to praise me for how I was a spitting image of Dad. "Every time I look into your eyes, I see your silly father," she'd say. But now, my eyes, adorned with the same gold flecks as his, complimented by our once-beloved smile, were a curse, a constant reminder of the man she loved. I guess death can do that, change beauty into ugliness in one swift moment.

"Good luck, Mom. I'm sure you'll get…." I began.

"Michael, you're late! Go catch the bus."

She walked over to the door and kicked it shut.

"The raise," I finished to the closed door. I lowered my head and trudged on. Glancing inside the pantry, I grabbed a strawberry Pop-Tart and a granola bar.

"Make sure you take the trash out before you go to school. And don't forget," she yelled from her room.

I shook my head. "I won't forget, Mom."

I crumbled the Pop-Tart's foiled wrapper and tossed it in the trash.

"Curry for the three," I said, high-fiving my imaginary fans.

Suddenly, my heart sank as the unmistakable sound of a school bus floated through the walls.

"Crap!"

I swung open the door and watched as the bus pulled away from the curb, disappearing down the street. I shut the door, pressing my back against it. I lowered my shoulders and sighed.

"Dang, it."

I swallowed.

"Mom, I missed the bus."

"Dang it, Michael Ethan Brown! Can't you do anything?" she roared behind the walls.

"Not like I did it on purpose," I mumbled.

I sunk into the couch and took a giant bite of my treat. Then, I slid my cell phone out of my pocket and quickly navigated to the chat app. My finger slid through my previous conversations until I reached Joshua's emoji, an image of Master Chief from Halo.

> "Yo, can you pick me up?"
> "lol, miss da bus again?"
> "Yeah."
> "Moms pissed?"
> "Yeah. Can you come get me?"
> "I got you. Be there in ten."
> "Ty."
> "Yep."

"Mom, I'm catching a ride," I yelled. She didn't respond, but I could feel her eyes rolling from here. I shook my head and slammed the rest of the Pop-Tart in my mouth.

CHAPTER FOUR
MICHAEL

"Thanks, man," I said, reaching over to buckle myself in. Since Priscilla's seat was so far back, I had to do this weird position where my legs were sprayed out. His car didn't accommodate taller individuals, and Priscilla didn't help the situation.

"Yeah, bro. I got you," he said.

The car jerked forward as music blasted from the speakers. Priscilla leaned forward and turned the music up, sending Eminem's "Darkness" rattling in my ears. Her shoulders shifted back and forth as she mouthed the words.

"Mom pissed?" Joshua said, staring at me from the rearview mirror.

"Of course. Always," I said.

"Want me to come over and put a smile on her face? Maybe she just needs a man in her life"

"Hey," Priscilla scowled, elbowing him.

"It was a joke. You know you're the only woman who can make me feel like a man."

"Such a jerk," she said. She twisted her body and gave me a pitying frown. "Sorry about your mom. That sucks."

"Yeah," I said.

I forced a smile but knew deep down I wasn't making it any easier on Mom either. I was always screwing up at home and at school. Joshua and Priscilla always wanted to ditch classes, and I couldn't not go, right? I mean, they wouldn't want to hang out with me if I didn't, and then where would I be? Maybe I could make Mom dinner or something. She'd like that, or at least, I think she would.

I leaned against the window and took in the view. The large elm trees arched over the street, their branches waving us on as we sped by. A woman in a black sedan used her knees to steer as she applied make-up with one hand and talked on her phone with the other. A string of minivans followed behind, turning onto Main Street, while bystanders stood at crosswalks, waiting patiently. The scent of freshly cooked cupcakes floated from Kia's Cupcakes. It was the best smell ever.

Reminiscences of the Oakview festival were still present. Flyers from last week's events were stapled to telephone poles as the wind gently pushed leaflets and glitter throughout the streets. The litter was, of course, despite the efforts of the community clean-up crew that pounded the pavement days after the festival.

Joshua's car slowed until it stopped a few feet from the intersection, meaning like ten feet away from the crosswalk. Joshua reached for the knob and lowered Joyner Lucas' voice to barely audible.

I glanced around, trying to figure out why he stopped so far back. There was nothing out of the ordinary. Nobody was trying to get from one side of the street to the other, so that wasn't it. The only car around close to us was a Honda Civic whose bass roared out, vibrating the vehicle with every beat.

The car peeled out once the light turned green, sending gas fumes flying in our direction. Joshua slowly eased his car into the intersection and then turned the music back up with a reach of his arm.

Lizzo's "It's About Damn Time" came alive from Priscilla's lap as she lifted her phone and rested it against her ear.

"Hey, girl. Yeah. No, we're coming now. Had to pick up Michael. Mom issues," she said. She lowered the phone and turned to Joshua.

"Madison?" Joshua asked.

"As usual," she mouthed.

He shook his head and kept driving.

"Okay, we just arrived. See you soon," Madison said, disconnecting her ear from the phone.

"What does the Queen want now?"

"Stop it." Priscilla smiled, pushing him jokingly against his arm.

"She just wanted to see where we were."

"Mmmhmmm," he said.

She turned to face me and smiled. I returned the smile. As Joshua scanned the street, looking for an opportunity to turn inside the school parking lot, Priscilla's smile lingered on mine. She glanced down at my lips and then back to my eyes.

I wasn't sure what to do, so I looked away. When I glanced back, she had already readjusted her position, and her eyes were all over Joshua.

CHAPTER FIVE
EMMA

The growling grew as my stomach churned. I rubbed my hand on my belly, trying to coax it to calm itself. I felt like vomiting would have been easier, but that wasn't an option. The uneasy feeling was becoming too frequent. It wasn't constant, but at times, it grew almost uncontrollably.

I stepped into the school and instantly felt eyes locking on me. The usual yelling and laughter were replaced by silence and soft mumbles between friends. I squeezed the straps on my backpack and kept walking. I knew my return since the car accident would raise some attention, but I never expected to feel like a caged animal in a zoo. Maybe if I held my head down, they wouldn't see me, and I wouldn't notice them.

Kids parted like I was Moses, which I didn't mind. It made walking to my locker much more accessible—no shoulder bumps and squeezing through circle of friends like usual. The distinct smell of perfume and cologne came to life as I walked along the walls lined with lockers. When I reached mine, I placed my books into my locker and leaned my head inside as far as it could go. Closing my eyes, I focused on my breathing.

"Maybe I should hide in here. I can survive the day like this," I thought.

A gentle tapping arose from the other side of my locker.

"Hey, Emma. Are you sure you want to come back to school? I mean, I'm sure the school would let you..."

"No, I want to come back. I'm fine. I just need everyone else to move on," I groaned.

"Oh wow, she's already back at school," a girl loudly whispered to her friends as they passed.

"Yeah, I definitely would have stayed home and milked the accident for as long as I could. I mean, it was her...," another girl chimed in, her words fading as they turned the corner.

"Yeah, I don't think that's going to happen," my best friend Zahra said. "So, you might as well just come on out."

I peered out of the locker and stared at Zahra. Her full name was Zahra Marie Baldwin, but I just called her Zahra. Her warm brown complexion and wavy black hair, which tiptoed atop her shoulders, highlighted her Persian roots; a gift from her mom. Meanwhile, her dad provided her mesmerizing green eyes, which she hid under thick-rimmed glasses.

Her plaid pajama bottoms with matching red Crocs screamed Zahra, while her faded navy-blue T-shirt showcased The Rock on the front. And by The Rock, I'm talking old-school eyebrows raised, "Smell what The Rock is cooking" old-school.

She leaned against the locker next to mine. Her arms were folded as she eyed everyone who walked by. I placed my hand on her shoulder.

"You don't have to be my guard dog. I'll be fine," I said.

Her face relaxed, and she glanced over at me, finally taking a breath.

"Fine," she said, raising her hands in defense. "I'll calm down, but the first time someone says something to you, girl, Imma..."

"I know, I know. Lay the smackdown. You really should update your catchphrase to something from this decade." I shot her a smile.

"Why change it if it's not broken? Plus, you know no one can mess with my girl," she said.

"Plus, I only have to last three days this week. That's it."

"Yeah, why come back on a Wednesday, anyways?"

"Because no one likes Mondays," I said.

"True."

"And if I return on a Tuesday, Tuesday becomes the new Monday. So, Wednesday it is." I shot her a smile.

"You're wise beyond your years, young grasshopper," she said, extending her arm for a high-five.

I paused and stared at the purplish-green ovals on her right bicep. I opened my mouth to speak, but my body jerked forward, slamming into the locker door.

"Hey, watch it," Zahra roared. I turned to find Madison Mayfield.

"Welcome back, Lucy Liu," she said over her shoulder as she continued her merry little way. Her gaggle of followers snickered as they passed by. First, Priscilla Smith and Joshua Johnson, then Michael Brown. Only one bothered to look at me as if I was a real person. Michael. But, of course, he didn't stop. He never stopped.

Zahra helped me up, collecting my notebook that flopped against the ground. We stared at Madison as she strolled away. I could feel my anger bellowing. I wanted to put her in her place, but instead, I turned away and stuffed my books into my backpack.

"Ignore Miss Silver Spoon over there. Racist prick," Zahra began. "And to think, we were all best friends in kindergarten. See what happens when daddy becomes CEO of the company? Think you can do whatever you want."

I pinched my lips, cramming more items into my bag.

"You, okay?" Zahra asked, a softer, more apologetic undertone silencing her usual energetic voice.

"Mmhmm."

"Emma, you know..." she began.

"I'm fine," I mumbled. From the corner of my eyes, I could sense she was watching me. But she eventually turned away and stared back at Madison and her friends, laughing and joking like we were only there for their amusement.

"I have to go," I said.

"But the bell didn't even..."

The bell cut her words off, and the school came alive again with the hustle and bustle of teenage life. Lockers slammed as shoes squeaked against the linoleum floor. I turned to walk to my class, but stopped.

"It's good to know you have my back," I said. "I'll see you after class."

Then I disappeared around the corner.

CHAPTER SIX
EMMA

    Before heading to class, I ducked into the bathroom as three girls pushed past me, leaving their cheap perfume lingering in the air. The place was empty, minus discarded paper towels sprawling across the floor. I stepped to the mirror and stared.

    My reflection revealed warm ivory-colored skin, a teardrop-shaped face, and hickory-smoked eyes. Those were my mother's eyes. When I was younger, people said I looked just like her. I never saw it until recently.

I had her eyes, nose, and smile. The majority of my features were products of my Hmong heritage. But my dad's blood did run in my veins.

The most noticeable trait was my height. My dad stood at 6'2" and I came in just under 5'10". Yeah, it's not typical for most Hmong Americans. I also inherited his snob nose and gentle personality, which I sometimes considered a curse. Gentle doesn't always win battles and causes you to be pushed around by people who think they own this school. I just wished I had the strength to stand up for myself for once.

I sighed as the image in the mirror did the same. Tears began to form in the corners of my eyes, but I wiped them away before they could fully materialize. I took several deep breaths and tried to calm myself. Madison always had this effect on me.

Exhaling, the tension ceased. I nodded as if I had just given a motivational speech and collected myself. I walked out the door and headed to class.

CHAPTER SEVEN
MICHAEL

"Bro, what should we do, man? I can't think of anything. Every time I come to this stupid class, my brain goes poof." Joshua made an explosion gesture with his hands against his temple.

He leaned back in his chair, tossing wadded-up paper into the air.

My eyes followed the paper as it went up and landed securely in his palms. I glanced over at the worksheet and reread the instructions.

Create an organization to help the local community and draft a mission, vision, and goals statement. All organizations must be original and must align with the school's values.

"What if," I paused, tapping the pencil on my head.

"Yeah," he said, leaning in my direction, eyebrows raised.

"Never mind, I got nothing," I finally finished.

"Bro," he said, defeated.

I scanned the room. Everyone else was hard at work. The other students' hands flashed through the page as their ideas flowed.

Amy and Zena were talking about a foundation for the blind. At the same time, Scott and Peter focused on a youth sports program.

I turned to the back of the class to Emma's seat. The sunlight from the window didn't quite reach to the back, so while others thrived in the brightness of the sun, the back corner seat, Emma's seat, was lit by a dim afterthought.

I watched as her head dove to the desk, but like it was planned, it lifted moments away from crashing. Emma stretched her eyes, trying to break the tiredness curse, just to recreate the same scene moments later. I smiled.

Seeing her brought back so many memories, with thoughts racing in my head. Emma was my best friend and, at times, my only friend. Besides my dad, she always saw me for me, not just a punching bag. She saw me as someone more, someone capable, even when all I saw was failure. She once said I could be a hero like my dad. When she said it, I shrugged it off, but honestly, I still lingered on those words to this day.

But now, even though we sat feet away, somehow, we seemed worlds apart. An emptiness slowly crept into the pit of my stomach. My smile quickly vanished, and I turned away.

I turned back to Joshua and stared at the paper but couldn't concentrate on the assignment.

"Hey, maybe after school, can we talk about something?" I asked. My voice seemed like it was coming from a thousand miles away.

"Oh man, I know what this is about."

He banged the front legs of his chair against the floor. Turning to me, he placed his hand on my shoulder.

"You know what it's about?" I said barely above a whisper, leaning forward.

"No wonder you've been acting strange. Yeah, man. I get it. You're...," Joshua paused as I leaned closer, hoping no one else would hear, "you're on your period."

His laugh rumbled the walls as students peered up in our direction. I shook my head and felt my temples straining.

"Such a jerk," I mumbled.

"Mr. Johnson, that is enough," Mr. Greene snapped. "Everyone, back to your assignments."

The rest of the class continued their projects, and Joshua returned to his solo game of catch. I stole a glance back at Emma. But unlike before, her eyes were locked on mine.

At that moment, my mind went back, back to when it was just her and me, back two years ago.

I rubbed my eyes, revealing a blurred city street below. My feet dangled from the rooftop as I took in a breath. I leaned forward, feeling gravity slowly pull me forward. Despite being only on the second floor, the ground looked miles away.

With clenched fists, I opened my mouth, but no screams emerged. Instead, the overpowering feeling of running blanketed my soul. I needed to run. Run fast, run far. I didn't care where to, I just wanted to run away from here and find a way to escape.

I needed to, my thoughts paused as the recognizable sound of my bedroom window sliding open and someone climbing out sprang to life. I didn't need to look at who it was. It was her.

I stared ahead as she lowered herself next to me. I turned slightly, watching as the sun covered her jeans with an orangish tint. As her feet joined mine, swinging above the ground, I took in another breath but didn't speak.

After several moments, she finally spoke.

"You, okay?"

"Mmhmm," I nodded.

"Want to…," she began.

"No."

I didn't want to talk about it. There was no point. The teasing lingered in my mind, on a constant loop. I was sick of it. Sick of all of it. Something had to change. I had to change.

She lowered her head and let out an audible sigh that somehow made me feel better. It let me know I wasn't alone, even though I thought that was what my heart truly wanted.

Emma understood me without words. She knew my struggles with bullying and constant feelings of inadequacy. She understood because she faced them too, through the continuous racial jabs and taunts. But she never gave in to them, not like me. Sure, she had her tough days, but around me, all I saw was her incredible strength. I envied her. I couldn't help but envy her, especially on days like this when the bullying devoured every sense of me, and the thought of facing the world seemed impossible.

I closed my eyes, shutting out the world. We sat there until the sun set beyond the horizon, leaving a dark purple afterglow filling the sky above.

The memory quickly faded as fast as it arrived, and I was back locked in her vision. I felt as if I didn't deserve to look into her precious brown eyes. But something inside of me had to force myself. This was wrong.

I wanted to tell her so many things. To tell her I was sorry for everything that happened between us. To tell her every piece of me died inside the second I stared into her eyes. To tell her losing her friendship was harder than losing my father.

I didn't expect her back so soon. I thought I would have more time to come up with something to say. Eventually, I broke away from her, leaving so many unsaid things lingering in the abyss.

"What about," I said, turning back to face Joshua, "an organization to help local animals? Like a shelter or something?"

"Sounds good, bro," he began, "if I wanted to fail."

He shook his head and leaned back on the rear legs of his chair, sending the paper ball into the air.

As we watched it fall, Mr. Greene quickly snatched it mid-flight.

"Hey, what the...," Joshua said, startled. His chair made a thunderous bang as it righted itself.

"That is enough, Mr. Johnson. Focus on your project. You need a good grade." He began to walk away but stopped and turned back around. "You'll need all the help you can get unless you want to spend all of summer with me."

Joshua grimaced. He mumbled something under his breath, but thankfully, neither I nor Mr. Greene understood him.

I turned to face my paper again and sighed. I should have picked a better partner.

CHAPTER EIGHT
EMMA

During class, Mr. Greene provided further instructions on our group project. We had been divided into groups of two, well, the rest of the class was. While others chatted with their partners, I sat by myself, one of the perks of having uneven students in class, I guess.

Mr. Greene allowed me to work with another group, a three-person team, but I chose not to. This way, I didn't have to convince anyone that my way was right or vice versa. It just seemed easier this way.

One thing that I didn't think about when I rejected his offer was that if I had a partner, they would be able to keep me awake during his lectures about business.

As his words slowly blended, I drifted asleep, forcing myself to balance my head before it plummeted to the desk. After several failed attempts and possibly a five-minute nap, I snuck my journal out of my backpack. My fingers roamed across the black leather exterior. The smell always brought a smile to my face.

My mom gave this to me when I was twelve. She noticed I wasn't having the best time at school or in life and thought it might help me relieve some stress. I was grateful she was so observant at times.

Most people wrote their thoughts and emotions, but I preferred to draw. There was something euphoric about sketching out my life. Ever since the car accident, it became my therapy. A way to uncage my mind and let it roam free. Maybe it was the smell of the lead or the sound of the pencil against the paper that soothed my soul. I didn't know. But for whatever reason, it helped.

I flipped to a random empty page, and my pencil danced against the canvas. The smell of lead floated from the paper as one shape morphed into another. I tilted the pencil as the lines grew darker. Blacks blended with grays as the page filled with life. Suddenly, the warmth of someone's gaze caught my attention. I looked up, and there he was.

Michael watched me as if I were Picasso or Rembrandt. His eyes took my mind back to when we were closer. I met his eyes, and for a moment, it felt like we were connected once more. Strangely, it felt good.

I quickly turned away and shook my head as if trying to wipe away the thought of us together. But how could I erase us when, in reality, there never was an "us," just a "me" and him, but never "us"?

Heat flowed through me, and my wrist twitched with life. Dots morphed into lines. Circles transformed into faces. Squares bloomed into bodies, and in the end, an image breathed life into the paper.

The bell rang, signaling the end of class. Kids got out of their seats and hurried out of the room. I was focused on the last bit of my artwork when Michael approached.

A breath escaped me as I took him in. His scruffy hair hung over his pecan-brown eyes. He stared down at my page. He lifted his eyebrows, and his eyes grew wide. He didn't speak. I sat there frozen, with no words, and the brief moment seemed to last lifetimes. He just nodded and slowly walked away.

I looked down. There, amongst the emptiness of the page, was a scene like no other. Scales covered a monster's large body as it sat perched, ready to attack. Its talons dug into the soil, and its tail pounded the ground. Fire roared through the blood-filled eyes as smoke bellowed around the dragon's body. But it was its facial features that would probably cause any double takes. Its face was that of a young girl. Madison.

I closed my journal and slid it into my backpack. As I gathered the rest of my belongings, my thoughts were consumed by the encounter with Michael. The idea of him inches away from me burnt my skin. Lost in my own thoughts, I made my way out of the classroom, joining the stream of students in the hallway. One class down, six more to go.

CHAPTER NINE
MICHAEL

After class, I fist-bumped Joshua as he headed to Geometry and went to A.P. Science. On my way, I saw my boy, Stanley, and walked over to him.

Stanley was somewhat of a local celebrity to the students. He was basically our in-house D.J. No party started until Stanley, also known as D.J. Panda Bear, was in the house. He was so cool.

I envied his skills, but honestly, it was the way he didn't have to try to be cool. Everyone loved him for him. Even without the music, he still carried himself as if he were comfortable in his own skin.

He could just walk up to anyone, and five minutes later, they would be best friends. I wasn't sure if it was his confidence or just his personality, but I was in awe of him. I could never do that. It took me forever to lose the stutter, and still, I had no confidence in how to speak. I never had that.

I often wondered what that felt like to be comfortable with who you were and have everyone know your name. I mean, I guess I had that now that I was hanging with Madison and Joshua, but I still yearned to have people know me for me. Even though, I still had no idea who I was.

I always wanted to be free enough to let people into my world, to let them see the real me. I wanted people to know I loved scary movies, reading fantasy books, and hiking. I dreamed of becoming a teacher or guidance counselor so I could help kids understand their true path in life before they reached my age. But deep down, I wanted...I wanted people to know that my smile was a mask I wore to hide the tidal wave of depression, drowning my self-esteem, robbing me of a chance to breathe, and truly feel alive. I wanted them to understand that I always felt like I might never be enough.

"Mikey Mike, what's good, bro?" Stanley said, scratching an imaginary record player in the air.

I smiled and clenched my hand in his.

"What's good, man?" I said.

"Nothing, about to do my Band thing."

"Why are you even taking Band? You're the best D.J. ever. You should be leading class, not going to some boring band class," I said.

"Nah, man. I love Band. Everyone thinks being a good D.J. is about turning a few records. But you need to know music. You have to love it."

I scrunched my face.

"Huh? I mean, I love music, too."

He laughed.

"Bro, I could mix a few tapes because I thought the music sounded good, right?" he said. By this time, his left hand was on my shoulder as his right accentuated his words in the air.

"Right. Right?" I said, not really knowing if I was asking or telling.

"My dude. Wrong! Being a good D.J. is about hearing the subtle changes with every beat of the instruments. When I do my thing, I hear the drums beat like elephants as they stomp through the pasture, or I hear," he closed his eyes, probably envisioning every beat, "I hear pixies dancing in the air as flutes serenade their dance."

I leaned in, closing my eyes, trying to feel what he felt, hear what he heard.

"I hear lions roar as the trumpet booms. Alligators snap their teeth as the symbols bang together."

He went silent. I opened my eyes and stared. After a few moments, his eyes reappeared, and the only way I could genuinely describe his expression was satisfied.

"Understand?" He smiled.

I nodded.

"Are you sure?" he asked, his smile widening.

With a gentle smile, I turned my head, hoping my face didn't reveal my embarrassment. Stanley let out this huge gut-driven laugh that echoed down the hall.

"Alright, man," he said between laughs, "I'll see you later. You coming to the party, bro? I have a few special tricks up my sleeve."

"Only if you're the D.J.," I said.

"Always, bro! I got you," he said, disappearing around the corner.

I waved as I headed to class, fighting the waves of other students.

CHAPTER TEN
EMMA

"Okay, take your left hand and raise it in the air," Ms. Rhodes said, instructing the first group of students. "Now…"

"Mrs. Rhodes, do I do the opposite if I'm left-handed?" Alexander said, struggling with the equipment.

The teacher rolled her eyes.

"Yes, Alexander, of course. Do the opposite."

I patiently waited in line. The first group continued. They grabbed their arrows and loaded them into the bow. Following the teacher's instructions, the area erupted with whooshes and thwapping sounds as students pulled back and released.

While some arrows went maybe ten yards, most fell at the shooter's feet.

A blood-curdling scream roared from my left. I turned to see Madison jumping back as her arrow flopped by her foot. I guess she feared the arrow would sever her pretty little manicured toes.

"That wouldn't be so bad if..." I shook off the thought before finishing the statement.

A few guys behind me snickered, expecting they would have done better. Madison turned, sneering at them. Their laughter was quickly replaced by quiet, obedient teens.

"You're definitely the supervillain in this comic book," I mumbled.

After a few more attempts and the multiple concussions Ms. Rhodes probably had from facepalming herself at the students' lack of ability to hit the target, she instructed the first group to place their bows back on the ground and proceed to the back of the line.

My group was next. I approached the line and waited. A strange tingle shot through my fingers as a warm cloud coursed through my body. I shook off my nerves and focused on the teacher.

Ms. Rhodes robotically repeated her instructions, and group two followed. When I picked up the first arrow, I clumsily slid it into position and pulled back. My arms shook from the unusual movement. Dang, this was harder than it looked.

"And fire," Ms. Rhodes commanded.

I released, sending my arrow flopping to the ground a few yards away. I waited for the audience to boo me off the stage, but thankfully, no one did. Maybe Madison was good for something after all. I quickly threw that idea out the window.

I reached for another arrow and lined myself up. When I looked down the field, I noticed a woman standing just beyond the target.

Grey streaks brushed her jet-black hair, which flowed over her shoulders. Wrinkles and scars etched along her face. Her eyes were sunken and screamed of a challenging life. The corners of her lips pressed down, as her midnight-black eyes stared directly at me. I looked at the other students. No one else seemed to notice her.

"Emma, shoot your arrow, please," Ms. Rhodes commanded. "Greg, do not point your arrow anywhere other than down the field."

I turned to Ms. Rhodes and was about to tell her about the woman, but when I looked back, she was gone.

"Emma!"

"Yes, ma'am," I said.

Maybe I was seeing things. I should have listened to the doctor and stayed home longer. But instead, I shook it off and lifted the bow.

I closed my right eye and then took a deep breath. The movement in my body slowed, seemingly freezing in time. I exhaled, and then my world suddenly vanished.

A vast forest clearing replaced the schoolyard. Monstrous trees walled the outskirts of the clearing. Birds with black heads and blue bodies soared through the sky as clouds danced in the background. While the sun hung directly above us, the smell of dirt and pine wafted in the air. A gentle breeze rippled strands of my hair against my cheek.

An older woman stood next to me. Her long midnight-black hair flowed over her shoulders. It was the same woman as before, but she was much younger. Earlier, she looked to be my grandmother's age, but now, she was maybe twenty, if that.

Adrenaline shot through me, and I felt like I couldn't breathe. A hint of nausea rushed over me as the woman's hand moved to mine. My eyes grew wide while she guided my left hand onto a bow. With her other arm, she reached around me, grabbing my right elbow.

"Head up," she said.

I swallowed. Her voice was strong yet felt comforting.

"Elbow back, like..."

She adjusted my elbow, ensuring it aligned with the arrow.

"Like this," she finished.

"One day, you will need this to fight for your people."

I turned my head to look at her, but she gestured down the field, where large, thick-rooted trees waited.

"Breathe," she ordered while readjusting my body.

I took a deep breath in. Her hands moved, one on my chest and the other on my back, as if examining my breathing. My heart regained its normal rhythm as I focused on her voice.

"Slower," she said.

My breathing gradually slowed. A weird calm rested inside me.

"You are now one with the arrow, and the arrow is now one with you," she said. "When the arrow soars through the sky, you fly as an eagle would fly towards its prey. Find your prey."

I took another breath.

"Be the eagle." Her voice was barely above a whisper. "Be the eagle."

I exhaled and with one fluid motion, released. The arrow flew through the sky, no, not the arrow, but me. I soared through the sky, stretching my wings and slicing through the air. Shadows danced between the trees, as the wind flickered against my skin.

The arrow landed securely inside the heart of the tree, crowded with several other arrows, other eagles that had found their prey. My eyes went wild, and the joy I felt was unreal.

"I did it," I mumbled as my thoughts scrambled, realizing what I had just accomplished.

"Yes, you did."

I looked up and saw a soft, knowing smile appear on her face.

"Now again," she commanded.

I grabbed another arrow, placed it in the bow, and took my position. She adjusted my body again, and like before, she rested her hands on my chest and back. I let out a deep breath, letting the rest of the world vanish, and again my eagle soared through the sky, nailing the tree once more.

"Again," she said, and again I reached back, grabbing another arrow.

I took my position and waited. I expected to feel her rough hands pressed against mine, but it never came. This time, she sat back and waited.

I situated my elbow further back, as she had adjusted it before. After a few deep breaths, I released the arrow, sending the eagle flying toward its target. Again, I hit the tree, but this time closer to the center.

She lifted her chin, and a thin-pressed smile appeared.

"Good," she said.

With her right hand, she lowered my bow and positioned me to face her.

"You must train like a warrior because you are a warrior. It flows in your bloodline, strong like a wild river," she said. "Look around you. This land is your land. These people," she motioned to the people behind us.

There were other people like her. Small children, with skin the color of burning sand, played and danced, while women with long, flowing black and gray hair carried wicker baskets from one hut to another. An older woman sat in front of a giant black pot, churning something with a large wooden stick, steam flowing from within.

Beads wrapped around their necks. Terry cloth covered their bodies as their bare feet pounded against the grass.

"This is our land, and people will come to take it from us. They are not one with nature. They are not one with us. So, we must fight. Do you understand me?"

I stared directly into her eyes. They pierced my soul as if she were tattooing her thoughts and fears directly onto my heart. An overpowering yearning to be loved drifted within me. I hadn't felt this in a while, a sense of belonging, the warmth of family.

"Yes, I understand," I said, nodding slowly.

"Good. Now again."

I positioned myself in front of the target, grabbed an arrow, and lined up. This time, no adjustment was needed. I released the arrow, and the world vanished once more.

When the darkness subsided, I was back at school. Thousands of eyes were now staring directly at me. I exhaled deeply, lowered the bow onto the grass, and stood.

My nerves sent electricity throughout my body as I caught my breath. I extended my fingers, trying to calm them from their shaky state.

The class erupted with hushed whispers as Ms. Rhodes walked over to me.

"Have you shot a bow and arrow before, Emma?"

"No, ma'am," I stuttered.

"That's some straight bullsh…." Madison began.

"That is enough, Ms. Johnson," Ms. Rhodes interrupted. She turned back to me.

"Then, can you explain this?"

She gestured to my target, which was punctured with four arrows, all aimed at the bullseye. I didn't even realize I had shot all my arrows besides the first one.

"I can't, ma'am. I can't explain it," I said. A flush crept across my cheeks as I lowered my head. I wrapped my arms around my body, concealing it from the world.

"So, you're telling me you've never shot before and got four bullseyes? Really?" she asked.

By this time, I felt the heat of embarrassment flow through me.

"Yes," I began. I cleared my throat. "Yes, ma'am," I said, more murmurs from the crowd behind me.

Ms. Rhodes stood there, studying me. She lifted her chin and instructed the students to line back up in their groups.

"Group 3, get ready."

I disappeared behind the lines, trying to make myself as small as possible. I had to get answers. My mind had to wrap around what had just happened. Was that a daydream, or did I really go to a forest? And who was that lady? She seemed so familiar.

CHAPTER ELEVEN
EMMA

"This is our land, and people will come to take it from us."

Her words echoed in my mind. It had to be real, right? I still felt everything: the wind brushing against my skin, the heat radiating from the sun, and the warmth in her eyes. I felt it all.

I had to find out if this was real. I skipped my usual after-PE shower and went back to the field. If I hurried, I still had time before the next class began.

When I arrived, I saw the carnage of class. Arrows sprawled across the grassy area. A dozen archery targets leaned as miniature holes punctured the red and blue covering. I scanned past the targets until my eyes rested on where the woman once stood.

"Where are you?" I whispered.

"Where are you?"

An overwhelming sense of confinement leaked into my subconscious, as if trapped within a cage. I squeezed my eyes shut as thoughts of the car accident came to life. Broken glass shattered, heat pressed against the contour of my skin, and screams rang out.

"No," I mumbled, shaking my mind free. With three slow, deliberate breaths, my thoughts cleared once again, and I refocused on the mission.

I wasn't sure what I thought was going to happen as my heart continued to throb. A part of me hoped to see her again. But another part, probably my more rational side, knew it was just a figment of my imagination. Crazy teenage hormones, probably.

My body jolted as the school bell rang, breaking my concentration. I shook my head and took one final look.

"So dumb," I muttered to myself as I turned to walk to class. "Hopefully, no one saw me out here, looking craz…"

I froze as heat floated over me, tracing the outlines of my skin. My heart pounded. Tiny hairs on the back of my neck perked up as the sensation of being watched rushed over me. I closed my eyes and swallowed, slowly turning around.

When the world came alive again, I stared into the vast, empty field. My eyes jumped from right to left and nothing. Upon realizing she wasn't there, my shoulders slumped, and I exhaled. I hadn't noticed I was even holding my breath.

"Forget this," I said, turning around. "If I hurry, I won't be late for class."

As I did, one word floated to my ears:

"Fight!"

CHAPTER TWELVE
MICHAEL

After school, I waved at Joshua and Priscilla as they drove off. The neighbor's labrador retriever, Pepsi, ran to the fence to greet me with drool-filled barks. He jumped up but flew back as his chain caught.

Letting out a little squeal, Pepsi adjusted himself and then stretched its body toward me. I smirked.

"Dumb dog."

I walked into the house, and a rotting odor slapped my face. My eyes widened, and I stepped outside, glancing at the curb. Empty trash bins lined the street in front of everyone's house except ours.

"Oh crap," I said. "Mom is going to go ballistic."

I shook my head as the door closed. I threw my backpack on the table and grabbed a snack.

I looked up at the wrapper.

"Good for breakfast, better for snacks." I ripped the wrapper and scarfed down the two Pop-Tarts.

After thirty minutes or so, keys jingled from outside the front door. I tucked my head in my book and bit my bottom lip.

"Uh, hey, Mom. How was…," I began.

She threw her keys on the side table. Her purse dropped to the floor, sending a thud ringing throughout the house. Her hair was messy, and her blouse was already untucked.

Mom stormed into the kitchen and disappeared around the corner. Cabinets slammed, and she let out very loud, exhausted breaths. Then, the room went silent. I closed my eyes and waited.

I wasn't sure what I wanted to happen. Maybe a night that started out differently. A night where Mom would come home after having a great day at work. Then, we would sit around the table, sharing laughs and secret inside jokes that only we shared. But that didn't happen. That never happened.

The silence was soon drowned out by a sound that had been etched in my subconscious. A sound that was as familiar to me as an "I love you" to a loving mother to her child. A sound that I've heard so much that sometimes I hear it even when it doesn't exist. I swallowed as the familiar sound of a bottle top popping off filled the room, like every single night before.

She stomped back into the living room and collapsed on the fabric loveseat.

"I guess you didn't get the raise," I said.

"Ya think?" she snapped, taking another long swig of her beer.

I grimaced as heat fluttered within me. Why did I just say that? So dumb. I knew how much this raise meant to her. If she could get it, then that meant more money. Maybe things around here would change. Perhaps she wouldn't be so angry all the time. I looked down and tried to focus on my assignment.

After about an hour, with Mom having made several more trips to the kitchen, I lifted my head and asked, "Want me to make dinner? We have a few T.V. dinners in the freezer."

She didn't respond.

"Mom?"

I turned to her, but she was already passed out. I snuck up to her and reached for the bottle, ensuring it didn't fall while she slept. But as I made contact, Mom gripped the bottle tighter and curled her body, never waking.

I picked up her shoes and placed them by the door. Afterward, I returned to the table and collected all my stuff, shoving them into my backpack. Then I tiptoed to my room.

With a few swipes of my thumb, my cellphone came alive, and I scrolled through social media. I liked a few pictures that popped up on my news feed. Priscilla posted a few selfies of her making a duck face while Joshua drove in the background.

Stanley posted about the upcoming party, highlighting his new playlist for the partygoers. Of course, we weren't dumb and knew our parents sometimes checked our accounts. So, we opted to use codes. His post read:

"Working on a new class project, and I'm guaranteed to get an A. I can't wait to show the class."

Thirty-nine people liked his post. I clicked and liked it as well. Then, I read the comments.

User FlyAzPhuq wrote: "Your class projects are always the best. I'll be there and I'm bringing extra pencils." This was code for "Your playlists are always the best. I'll be there, and I'm bringing rum."

User DonkeyKong24 wrote: "A plus plus plus."

Even Joshua got in on the action. He replied, "I've got pencils, pens, and a few binders. Let's do this," meaning,

"I've got rum, vodka, and a little tequila. Let's do this." I liked his comment.

After a few more minutes of browsing my news feed, I clicked on my profile and scrolled down to my photos. My face lit up as an image of me, Joshua, Priscilla, and Madison, appeared. It was at the last school pep rally, and we pretended to be dead from boredom. My smile faded as I noticed that a few rows behind us sat Emma and Zahra. Zahra was leaning into Emma as a delicate smile pressed against Emma's lips. Shared inside jokes that I was no longer privy to.

I swallowed and kept scrolling. There were a few more images of us at school, then a few I took at Kia's Cupcakes. I held my Strawverry Shortcake inches away from my opened mouth, with the caption "Party in my mouth!"

My heart sank when I saw a picture of me and my dad. His military hat, which he called a combination cover, sat tilted on my head as I rendered the best hand salute an eight-year-old could muster. He stood across from me, returning the salute. His eyes were red, and large bags resided under them. Still, he gave me a massive smile while folks in the background celebrated their family member's accomplishments as the United States Navy's newest Chief Petty Officers.

Mom and I got to go on stage and pin his new military rank on his uniform. As we approached, Dad knelt, allowing me to reach his shoulders. The new rank was a small golden anchor, which I slid onto the right shoulder of his khaki uniform, just as Mom did on the other shoulder. When he stood, tears roamed across his trembling cheeks.

He turned to Mom and planted a huge kiss on her, and then turned to me. Pulling me into him, I wrapped my arms around him and squeezed. Now, I wished I never let go of that hug. Maybe he would still be around if I hadn't.

The memory of that day brought a smile to my face. Dad was so happy, and Mom was too. She was so proud of him. Even though I was young, I remembered feeling this electricity in the air. Not from all the military members, but from the love and joy between us in that moment. It felt like home.

The caption read, "You will forever be my hero. I miss you, Dad." Forty-nine people liked it.

My thumb slung through the pictures, skipping them by 5s and 10s. When the screen stopped, another image captured my attention. It was an image of Emma and me posing on my roof, our usual hangout spot.

I leaned in and focused on something I hadn't noticed before. While I stared intently at the camera, grinning from ear to ear, Emma was staring at me.

We had been friends since we were six, but the look she gave me read something different, something more. Her brown eyes stared at me like I was the only person who existed. Her eyes were longing for something, but I couldn't tell what. I couldn't believe I never noticed that before.

"Whatever, Michael. You're going crazy," I told myself, shaking the thoughts out of my head.

I threw my phone on the nightstand and leaned against the bed as my head sunk into the pillow.

I jerked up. My eyes opened, revealing a dark and quiet room. It would have been deathly silent except for the buzzing of a fly banging himself against my window, searching for an escape. I threw my feet over the bed and reached for my phone. 12:47.

I extended my chest forward, stretching out my arms. I began to stand but paused. I woke up too soon. I had wished my dream would have lasted forever.

In my dream, I was a little kid, and Mom was chasing me around the house. Our hearty laughter echoed throughout the house, blending like the sweetest poetry. I ran into the living room, where Dad waited with open arms. With a leap, I was wrapped in his warmth, as he covered me like a blanket. As Mom turned the corner, her face radiated with life, causing everything inside of me to tingle. At that moment, everything was okay, and their love enveloped our home.

I stood as bits of my dream slowly faded from my memory. I never understood why dreams seemed to last forever but faded like brief glimpses of time the second the real world came alive again. I exhaled a giant breath as I slunk through the hall.

Mom looked as if she hadn't moved at all, but the collection of empty bottles said otherwise. Her body curled into the loveseat. The throw blanket partially covered her small frame.

I stared at my mom. Dark brown hair blanketed the side of her face, which had a blueish-purple tint, the effects of the television screen. Her left eye remained partially opened, revealing a color that resembled honey. My dad used to say her eyes reminded him of coffee because he could stay awake for days just staring into them. I wasn't sure if that was a bad dad joke, but Mom loved it when he said that.

I tiptoed over to her, grabbing the remote. Clicking the television off, I slowly placed it back on the loveseat armrest. Mom stirred momentarily, causing me to freeze, but thankfully, she didn't wake. When I stood up, I stared at her again and swallowed.

I slammed my eyes shut. My breaths were shallow, and my shoulders slumped. Tears formed at the corner of my eyes, but I didn't allow them to fall. Instead, I slowly walked back to my room, and went back to bed.

CHAPTER THIRTEEN
MICHAEL

"Oh my God, Ms. Martinez is the absolute worst. And I can't even understand her most of the time," Madison said.

I narrowed my eyes as my lip twitched.

"Oh, don't give me that look, Mr. Goodie Goodie," she said, "I mean because of the way she talks, not her foreign accent."

"But it's Spanish class," I said barely above a whisper.

Priscilla shot me a smile but quickly joined Madison, sitting on the top of the table. I hated when people did that. People ate there, and now their food would smell like... never mind.

I leaned against the adjacent wall as we waited for Joshua to arrive.

"Donde llama Madison," Madison said in the worst Mexican accent ever.

"I think it's Mi llama Madison," Priscilla corrected, which was met by a set of rolled eyes.

"I mean, I think. I don't really speak Mexican," Priscilla said.

"Mexican is a country, sweety. The language is Spanish. See? I am learning something in el bano," Madison said proudly.

"That means…." I shook it off. I didn't have the energy even to bother.

"What up, fools?" Joshua said, waving his arms in the air.

"Baby!" Priscilla said, running into his arms.

I turned my head as their lips met. Based on experience, I knew this would take a good two minutes. And it wasn't the sexy Spiderman and Zendaya type of kiss. It was more like the reunited Jennifer Lopez and Ben Affleck type, where yeah, it's cool, but he makes it seem creepy.

117. 118. 119. 120. Okay, and turn.

When I turned, their lips were still very much pressed against each other. Drool oozed out of the side of Joshua's mouth as their faces twisted and turned erratically. I forced a bit of vomit to stay subsurface and rode out the horrific wave until he finally pulled away from her.

They turned and watched as Madison climbed off the table.

"Hey, Joshua," I said, motioning him over.

"Bro, can't you see I'm with my lady?"

"Uh, yeah. I see that. But come here," I said.

He leaned his head back, exaggerating as if he was a little kid and his mom told him to go to his room. But thankfully, he slowly walked over.

"Bro, we need to talk," I said. My tone was rushed but below the hearing range of the two ladies.

"About?" he said, blowing kisses in Priscilla's direction.

"Did you not see Emma is back?"

"Emma?" he asked.

"Yeah, Emma, dude. We have to talk about," I paused, checking over my shoulder, ensuring no one could hear, "the party."

"Oh, yeah. Well, tell her, I said...wait, who's Emma?"

"Joshua!"

"Okay, calm down. Lucy Liu got it," he said.

"Quit calling her that. Lucy Liu's family is from Taiwan. Emma is Hmong," I yelled through whispered tones.

"Tomato, tomato, fried rice," Joshua joked. He then spent a minute laughing at his own joke, which he only interrupted by repeatedly asking me, "Do you get it?"

I pinched my lips and forced steady, even breaths. My body tensed, but I had to relax. Sadly, I needed Joshua; if I ruined this, if I didn't make it right by her, then I didn't know what to do.

"Joshua, please," I said.

"Okay, my bad," he said, putting up his hands in defense. "The floor is yours."

"I need you to..."

"Hey, are you love birds done over there? I'm hungry," Madison roared.

"Yeah, I'm hungry too, Baby," Priscilla added.

"Pizza!" Joshua yelled, running back over to her.

I banged my head against the wall. My fingers tapped against my sides as I shook my head.

"Unbelievable. Freaking unbelievable," I mumbled.

"Michael, you coming?" Priscilla asked.

I exhaled.

"I'll meet you inside."

CHAPTER FOURTEEN
EMMA

As I headed toward the parking lot, Amy Spitz caught my attention. She walked down the stairs, stuck up her finger as if she had just realized she had forgotten something, and then proceeded back up the steps. She disappeared around the corner. I raised my eyebrows and then kept moving.

I stepped through the school exit, and a sudden relief washed over me. I didn't know if it was the fresh, crisp air that splashed against my skin, the heat radiating from the beautiful, clear sky above, or maybe the fact that school was officially done for the day. Whatever it was, it felt great.

I sucked in the air as gas fumes from the nearby buses

floated into my nose. I wrinkled my face and tried to focus on the brighter things in life, like how the school day was done. My daydream was interrupted as an arm wrapped around my neck.

"Boo," Zahra shouted directly in my ear.

I bumped my head against hers.

"What's up, lady?" I said.

"So, guess who's going to a party this weekend?" she asked.

"Uh... Beyonce and Jay-Z?"

She shook her head.

"Us," she said, grinning from ear to ear.

"We don't do parties anymore. Remember, we're part of the anti-social community. All we do is make fun of people who go to parties," I said.

By this time, we both had stopped walking as other students rushed out of the school. Some piled inside school buses, while others hopped in waiting vehicles. Several students slid inside their cars as their friends piled in the back. Zahra and I were part of the third group.

Thankfully, Zahra had her own ride. It was a 1999 Nissan Frontier, which she lovingly called The Beast. To be honest, it should have been called The Beast That Sometimes Didn't Run.

We loved her truck, though. We usually spent nights in the bed of The Beast, staring at the stars or daydreaming about escaping our small town. We had our future already planned, since we were younger.

Zahra was going to major in neuroscience and minor in sports broadcasting. After graduating summa cum laude, she would discover a cure for dementia, a condition very close to both our hearts. Of course, she would marry a famous wrestler, whose name was now banned from The Beast because it was mentioned way too many times. We couldn't even play rock-paper-scissors anymore.

Eventually, Zahra and her man would direct a best-selling movie about how they met. Taylor Swift would play her, because who doesn't love Taylor Swift, and Kevin Hart would play him. Think rom-com, with a lot of wrestling action scenes. Zahra had it all planned out.

While my best friend's life was filled with glitz and glamour, my future life was more subdued. First, I'd wake each morning in my modest villa in Puerto Rico along the beach. The sound of crashing waves accompanied by serenading bananaquit birds and the chorus of coqui frogs would greet me each day.

I had a modest garden filled with papayas and cilantro, a peaceful retreat where I could wind down after a fulfilling day at Sweet Haven, my small yet thriving bakery. As people walked in, they would be enveloped by the aroma of freshly baked cupcakes. With every bite, they would be transported back to their childhood, making them feel like they were home again. Everyone deserved to experience that sense of belonging, even if it was just momentarily through a cupcake. Perhaps, by creating these moments for others, I, too, could find my own sense of fulfillment and belonging.

During hurricane season, I would fly back to the mainland to visit my kids, Zahra, Zander, and Zoey, and their kids, my grandbabies, who were my oxygen. And despite them complaining about hugging their mom and grandma, they would know that they were loved because I would tell them with every phone call, every visit, every hug. They would know. That would be enough for me.

That was all we wanted. To be honest, we knew if we stayed here after high school, we'd likely be stuck, unhappy, and probably in a loveless marriage, like many others. Thoughts of my parents drifted into my mind, but I quickly pushed them away. Plus, after the car accident, I felt less of myself, like something inside of me just wasn't the same and maybe leaving here would revitalize me, make me whole again.

The Beast fired up, and the radio blasted from the speakers. With some elbow grease, the window slid down, and the truck filled with the same crisp air that calmed my mind. And with that, we were off.

Our bodies jerked as Zahra shifted gears, pulling out of the school parking lot. Our heads bobbed with every beat, and I tapped my fingers against the rusted black exterior.

"So," Zahra began shouting above the sound of Miley Cyrus serenading us, "about the party, you want to go?"

I stared at her, between strands of my hair wrestling in the air.

"I don't do parties anymore," I screamed back.

She glanced at me and shook her head. She tapped the button, and the radio shrunk to barely inaudible.

"It'll just be that one time. Plus, you need to get out of the house. Ever since the accident..."

"Zahra," I screamed.

My body jerked forward as The Beast came to a sudden halt. My head slammed against the seat as the vehicle finally settled. I looked up, noticing the red light.

"Sorry," she said, twisting her face.

The screeching caught the attention of people on the streets. An older man stared wide-eyed as he jumped backward while trying to cross the crosswalk. A bald man in an orange robe stood across the street, staring at The Beast. His face didn't show emotion, just like a monk should be. That was a contrast to the UPS driver next to us, who twisted his face and stared us down as if he were scolding us with his eyes.

Zahra was my best friend, but she was the absolute worst when it came to driving. But she was the one with the car, er, the one with the truck, and she never let anyone drive The Beast. I was excited when she got her driver's license last year, but my excitement soon turned to a life of whiplash and motion sickness.

"Why do you want to go to a party? You hate people. I hate people. See? That's what we do. We hate people together," I said while rubbing the back of my neck.

She shifted the gears as The Beast jerked forward, then back. I stared outside as I followed a single snowflake that floated from above and landed perfectly on my arm. I looked up, but there were no clouds, just that single snowflake. Weird.

"I think you need to get out. Yes, we both hate people, but I think you need to live. We both need to live our lives." She paused as her mind wandered. "Life's too short. Plus, this is our last year of high school. Let's make the most of it so we won't regret it later."

I thought for a moment. There was something lying dormant inside of me, that refused to let me free from the shadows. But I couldn't let it take hold. I couldn't live in fear forever. Maybe this was the first step of starting anew. If I could do this, then maybe I could just survive the rest of high school.

"Fine," I said.

Her eyes widened.

"Really?" Her tone wasn't a happy surprise. It was more like an 'I thought you'd never say yes' surprise.

I nodded and gave my best attempt at a smile. It didn't work. My body jerked back as The Beast floated through the intersection—more whiplash.

"So hey, what happened with you at P.E.? People were calling you the Asian Robin Hood," Zahra said, pulling out of the intersection.

"Why do people have to say Asian?" I asked. "Why can't they just say Robin Hood?" I shook my head.

"Okay, Robin Hood. What happened?" she asked.

"I don't know. It was so weird. Like I was here one minute and the next I was..." I stopped myself as I peered over at her.

She glanced over and then back at the street.

"Well?" she said. "Spill it, tots!"

"Promise not to laugh?" I asked.

"Not at all. I make no promises. Just tell me what happened, then I'll laugh, then you'll laugh, and then Dwayne Johnson will come and carry me in his arms."

I stared at her.

"Stalk much?" I asked.

Her hand flew through the air, smacking me on my elbow.

"Tell me already."

"Fine. Fine." I blew out a slow breath and told her everything—the old lady, the forest, arrows, everything.

At first, she didn't speak. Instead, she would steal glances in my direction and then focus back on the road.

"Has this happened before?" she finally asked.

"No, first time."

She thought for a moment as she pursed her lips.

"Could this be related to...," she paused, shaking her head. "Could this be like a head trauma thing? You know, from the accident?"

I stared at her. I hadn't thought about it. Heck, it just happened, so I didn't really come up with other solutions because of the whole "I'm going crazy" part.

Maybe it was from the accident, but honestly, I barely remembered it, besides being hit by a truck and getting flipped over. That was about it. The doctor said I was concussed, which explained the memory loss. Dad said I just needed time to fully heal, and mom, well, mom had her own issues going on.

"Yeah, maybe."

Leaning against the window, I stared out at our small town. Oakview was the kind of place where you spent your entire life with the kids down your block. Yep, from kindergarten until marriage for some, and no part of me wanted to spend the rest of my life with the likes of Madison and Joshua.

Oakview was tucked between the Mississippi River and a whole lot of farmland. We had our share of parks, but the largest was on Elm Street. It wasn't unusual to see gangs of 8-year-olds with matching jerseys sprinting down the field, kicking soccer balls, and tripping over their own shadows. The parents would cheer on the sidelines while sneaking sips of beer between plays.

If you were lucky and the wind hit just right, the fantastic aroma from the local bread company would blanket the city, having everyone crave freshly baked bread. I'm glad I wasn't allergic to gluten on those days.

"What if," she began, "the accident caused you to have telepathic mental superpowers? How freaking cool would that be?" she said.

"Absolutely not," I said.

"Oh my God, you could be the next Avenger," she said excitedly.

"I mean, that would be cool, but I don't think the Avengers are real."

"Yeah, they wouldn't be until you joined the team," Zahra said.

I placed my hand on her shoulder.

"It's a good thing you're beautiful because..." I said, scrunching up my face.

"Thanks, well, I try. Wait... hey!" she said, finally catching the hint. "Hey, ever since you got superpowers, you have changed."

"It's not a superpower. Everyone will think I'm freaking crazy. I have enough on my plate to worry about," I said. I shifted, pressing my shoulder against the window again.

Birds played tag in the air as clouds hung perfectly still in the background. The smell of pastries floated into the truck as we passed Kia's Cupcakes. I swear I could taste their strawberry shortcake cupcakes, or as Kia calls them, her Straw-very Delicious.

"*Az Sar Rah Behro Birun*! Get out of the way," she waved her hand at the car in front of her, which was apparently taking too long to switch lanes.

"So, who was the lady in your vision?" she asked.

"I'm not sure, but I think," I paused, "I think she was my mom or something."

Zahra's eyes widened but she didn't look away from the road, thankfully.

"Your mom, like your real mom?"

"No, she was the person I was 'mom,' I mean, the person who I was, that was her mom. Oh my gosh," I growled, unable to explain it appropriately.

"Okay, got it," Zahra said. "How do you know it was the mom?"

I looked down, biting the bottom of my lip.

"I just knew. It felt like I was with my mom, ya know? Here," I said, pointing to my chest. "It felt like mom."

61

"Okay," she said, nodding in agreement. She let out an audible sigh. "Dang."

"Anyway, my mom—her mom—was teaching me how to shoot an arrow, and then she said I had to protect our people."

"From what?" Zahra said, turning into my driveway.

"I'm not sure." I looked at her face and saw her concern as if it reflected my thoughts.

"Divaneh. Crazy!" she mumbled.

"Yeah," I said.

"Are you okay? Like, are you really okay? I'm worried about you, Em."

Was I okay? I had no way of answering that question. I didn't know what any of it meant. A tightness flared in my chest as my mind felt trapped. Trapped between reality and whatever this was.

Zahra turned the key, sending The Beast into a sudden hibernation.

"If you don't want to go to the party, we don't have to. I just thought it would be good, ya know?"

I forgot all about the party. I agreed to go, but I doubted if it was the right decision. I didn't trust parties. I didn't trust people. Her house was safe. My house was safe. Parties were the opposite of safe.

I nodded, even though my mind wanted desperately to say no. She studied me, scrutinizing every inch of my face.

"You almost died, Em," she said, her voice cracking as tears welled in the corners of her eyes. "I thought you were gone, and watching you in the hospital was like," she paused, seemingly unable to finish her thought.

"It broke my heart watching your dad with your mom." She paused, squeezing her eyes shut. Her jaw trembled with every breath. "It just scared me."

Her head twisted as if kicking the negative thoughts out of her mind.

"I…"

She lifted her finger in the air, silencing me. After a few deep breaths, she continued.

"And it made me think, like, I don't want to die without truly living."

She turned away, as if the memories were flooding back to her, and she couldn't meet my gaze.

My mouth gaped, and my eyes fell upon my best friend. I hadn't realized the impact of the accident on her until now. And she was my best friend. My heart ached for her, knowing the worry she must have experienced. I swallowed.

"I guess we can't be anti-social, non-party people forever, right?" I shrugged.

She turned back and stared into my eyes.

"Right," she said and nodded.

CHAPTER FIFTEEN
MICHAEL

The following morning, I walked out into the living room and Mom was still where I left her. I stepped into the kitchen and headed to the refrigerator. There wasn't much in there, but we had enough. I grabbed the eggs and remaining bacon and went to work.

After a few minutes, the smell of the bacon blanketed the space, and the food was all done. I slid the eggs, bacon, and toast onto the plates. I heard her stirring when I reached over to dash salt on the eggs.

I walked over to the table and slid the plates onto the table. I looked over. Mom was rubbing her eyes as she stretched out.

"What time is it?"

"It's around 6:30, Mom. I know you had a bad day, so I figured I'd make you breakfast."

She leaned forward, twisting her body to peer up at the table. Without saying a word, she went to the table and plopped down. Mom stared at the plate for a minute and then glanced at me.

"Thanks."

Her voice was hoarse, which was expected after a night of drinking. I smiled and began to eat.

We didn't speak. Instead, our forks clinked against the plates, filling the silence as the taste of bacon splashed against our taste buds. I wasn't the best cook, but I could do breakfast.

She placed her fork down and rubbed the back of her neck. Her mouth opened to speak but quickly closed as if hesitant to talk to me.

"Uh," she began. "I'm sorry." Mom glanced up but quickly looked back down when our eyes met.

I studied her for a second, as my mind raced. She had never apologized for anything before. For that brief moment, my mom was back. The mom who cared about my feelings more than her own. The mom who yearned to make me smile. The mom who loved me.

There was so much I wanted to say, "Mom, I know how hard life has been, and I'm sorry. Mom, I'm here for you and always will be. Mom, I miss him too!" But that didn't come out. None of it did. Instead, all I said was, "It's okay."

She went back to eating, and I did the same. Moments later, she sniffed the air.

"Did you take the trash out yesterday?"

I peered up. Mom held her fork inches from the plate as she stared down at her food.

My shoulders slumped, and I just sat staring at my empty plate.

"Sorry, Mom. I'll do better next time."

As she raised her shaking head, I strained to catch the

mumbling words seeping between her lips.

"Always something."

Her body tensed and she glared at me. With every second, I felt more unspoken daggers piercing my soul until, eventually, her hatred had shrunken me to almost oblivion. My real mom, who hated every breath I took, was back. Of course, she was. She never really left.

We spent the rest of the morning apart. Mom needed her "alone" time. I spent the rest of the morning cleaning the house. After doing the dishes, I swept the floor and vacuumed the living room. Mom came in a few times while I was cleaning. She wouldn't say anything; she grabbed a few things and returned to her room. I could hear the television from behind the door.

After I finished, the house smelled like lemon, and I had just enough time to make it to school.

CHAPTER SIXTEEN
EMMA

    I walked into our house, and my mom stood in the corner, staring out the window. Streaks of light and shadows highlighted her light brown skin. Her deep brown eyes reflected the brightest of the day, although the room was dark and cold.

    My mom, Shoua Lee-Thomas, was born in Laos but spent most of her early years in Thailand. When she was eight, her mother (my tais-tais) and seven siblings came to the States.

    They risked everything to escape an abusive father and an even more violent government. My mom would often talk about what she remembered, and my uncles and aunts would fill in the gaps. It was amazing to hear about her life then and see her life now so drastically different.

My people, well, half of my people, were Hmong and survivors. Many were forced into the forests, escaping death at the hands of the guerrillas. Most migrated to America and brought their traits with them, as well as their culture. My uncles would tell me how they would buy houses with basements and fill them with water to harvest fish.

I wasn't sure if that was just a story an uncle would tell his naïve niece. Still, Mom often told me about sitting in the basement and watching the colorful fish dance like ballerinas, or at least what she imagined ballerinas would dance like.

But now, when she spoke of her childhood, a certain sadness came with the memories, a certain emptiness. My mom and Uncle Peter in Minnesota are the only living relatives on that side of our family left. Well, there's me. I never had siblings, but I couldn't imagine life without my parents or Zahra. Although she wasn't blood, she was family.

I dropped my bag and walked over to her. She stood like a statue, staring.

"Hey, Mom," I whispered, "I'm home."

She didn't speak, just stood there, staring at the outside world.

"Did you eat?" I asked, walking next to her. I leaned over her shoulder, peering out the window. "Mom, you know the neighbors will think you're a peeping Tom or something," I joked but neither of us laughed.

She didn't respond, she just kept staring.

I had read that a traumatic event could cause grave damage to one's mind. For me, it was memory loss, but for her, it was something more, something deeper. She hadn't been the same since the accident, and I feared she'd never return to her old self. It felt as if her body was here, but her mind, her soul was lost.

As my eyes roamed across her still body, I didn't know what to say or do. I had tried speaking with her countless times, but it always ended with her continuous obsession with staring out the window and my subsequent heartbreak. She just wasn't herself anymore. Her light was just a bit dimmer.

I wrapped my arms around her and felt her warmth. She smelled like a rose dipped in citrus, her favorite Valentino perfume. Usually, she only wore that on special occasions, but now it seemed like she wore it daily. Maybe I should have been grateful she was still taking care of herself. Perhaps she just wanted to smell and feel pretty.

I leaned in and kissed her cheek. Then, I headed to my room to start my homework. I had a feeling she'd still be there whenever I finished, still staring.

CHAPTER SEVENTEEN
MICHAEL

I headed to Joshua's party. He had been blowing me off for the last few days, and it was getting old. I had to say something. I needed his help with resolving things with Emma. If I couldn't fix this, then, well, I feared our friendship would only live on in my memories.

When I arrived, the party was already in full swing. I walked over to Stanley and gave him a fist bump. He bumped my hand and went back to sliding the tips of his fingers on the black records. He pressed his head against his shoulder, ensuring his headphones didn't fall off. With one smooth motion, his hand flipped off the record, sending the crowd erupting with "yeah" and, "Oh, this is my song."

I waved my fist in the air and proceeded to the kitchen. Nope, Joshua wasn't in there. I walked through the house. Halls held pictures of Joshua as a young boy. I guess he always had that devilish smile. The pictures of him as an older kid must have been in another part of the house because this only held images of him until maybe nine years old.

"Where is he?" I whispered to the vacant halls and empty bedrooms.

I froze.

"I need this," I told myself.

I had to find him. If I had to drag him with me, then so be it. Either way, we were coming clean to Emma. It shouldn't have happened. It was wrong, and it was all my fault.

I began to turn around and run out the door when someone called his name. As usual, I turned to find him chugging something from a red cup, probably party punch. I took a deep breath and headed toward him.

"Hey, can we...," I began.

"Heyyyyy, Mikey Mike in da house," he yelled while grabbing my neck, folding me in half. My head jerked back and forth as his words slurred.

He stood up and leaned closer to his ear.

"Can we talk?" I said, practically yelling.

"What?" he yelled back.

The music blared through the speakers next to us, making any conversation nearly impossible. I pointed to him and then to myself and moved my hands in a flapping motion.

"Can we talk?" I yelled slowly, exaggerating my mouth.

He looked down at the bottom of his cup and begrudgingly nodded.

"Let's go outside," I yelled.

He shrugged.

"Outside," I said, motioning to the door.

The music dimmed when we stepped out the door, and my hearing slowly returned. Joshua led me over to the garage, away from drunken partygoers.

"What's up?" he said.

"Joshua, you have to tell people what happened that night," I pleaded.

He nodded and began looking around as if I was wasting his time.

"What night, again?" he asked.

"Seriously?" I asked.

"I'm kidding, bro, relax. Get a drink. You need to breathe, man."

I could feel anger boiling inside of me. Was this guy serious?

"Listen," he began, "I don't know what you're talking about, bro. Lucy doesn't even know you're alive, so I wouldn't worry about it."

"Stop calling her…."

"Baby! Oh, hey, Michael." Priscilla walked over, extending her arm as Joshua scooped her up. The two exchanged another extended kiss, filling with hands roaming everywhere.

"What's good, Beautiful?"

"This party is off the chain, Baby."

"Well, you know how I do," Joshua said, almost stumbling over his own feet.

"Dang, we need to hurry up and get drunk," Priscilla said. Suddenly, Madison walked up to the group.

"No, Joshua's house. Yeah, bring rum."

She stuck up a finger and then pointed to her ear.

"Okay, yes, bring her! I love her. But not him. He has like major creep vibes."

She glanced at Priscilla and mouthed, "Jeremy." Priscilla shriveled her face as if she just got a whiff of something gross.

"Bye," Madison finally said, switching off her earbuds.

"Great party, Joshua. Better than the last one. See? I knew there was hope for you, yet."

Joshua did a fake laugh and began tripping over his feet again.

I took in the scene while the three talked. The bass of Megan Thee Stallion's "Dance" rattled the walls of the house as tons of kids I recognized from school piled inside. A gentle breeze danced between the trees, while red Solo cups littered the grass below.

My body jerked to the side as Joshua nudged me, leaning into me.

"Bro, wipe your drool. The hot one is mine," he said, ensuring his voice was low enough so Priscilla wouldn't hear him.

"What?"

"Zahra's looking good, bro," he whispered.

He gestured down the street, and I followed his line of sight. My heart nearly stopped when I saw two girls approaching. It was her. Emma.

CHAPTER EIGHTEEN
EMMA

"I can't believe you talked me into this," I said as I walked arm-in-arm with Zahra.

"You need to get out, girl. I'm pretty sure watching *Golden Girls* at home every night is getting old."

"*Golden Girls*? Why would you think I'm watching *Golden Girls*?" I asked, scrunching my face.

She laughed.

"You look like a Betty White type of girl. Just saying."

She squeezed my arm tighter as the crisp night air stabbed at our uncovered skin.

"Okay, but I'm staying by you the entire time, so

don't...," I began.

"Don't go running off with any boys," she finished. "Girls?"

"Zahra Marie Baldwin!"

"Just kidding. You didn't have to use my government name, Mom. I'll be your shadow all night," she said.

I guess my hermit life was officially over. But I couldn't lie. I was a little grateful to leave the house, even though I enjoyed my nights with Blanche and the girls.

"Whose party are we going to anyway?" I asked.

We rounded the corner of Central and Park Avenue. The neighborhood was asleep. Large elm trees umbrellaed the street, providing a cozy feel to the road. Houses were still, dark, with no movement. All except one.

People poured into a large white house. Upon recognizing it, the hairs on the back of my neck stood, and a prickling coursed through my arm.

"Joshua Johnson?" I said. I knew if Joshua was there, Madison and Michael would be there too. Two people I really didn't want to see.

My movement stopped, and my head instantly began to shake. A dread came over me as my body began to shake.

"I know you don't like parties, but what's up? Why are you shaking?" Zahra asked.

I stood there, frozen. She wrapped her hands around my wrist and slowly turned me to face her.

"Hey. What's going on?"

"I um...," I stuttered. I had never told Zahra the truth about my falling out with Michael. Hell, I never told anyone. Only one person truly knew my secret, and the weight of it all was paralyzing.

"There's something I didn't tell you," I said. I wiped the tears away as I stared into her gorgeous green eyes.

"Azizam," she said, rubbing my tears away. "What is it?"

"Remember when you went home to see your grandpa in the hospital?"

She nodded.

"Well, something happened here, and uh..."

My breathing shuttered. The tears roamed down my cheeks, and a heaviness consumed me.

Zahra wrapped me in her arms. Her lips pressed against my cheek as she held me.

"It's okay. You're okay," she said, seemingly knowing my pain before I could express it.

She peeled herself away from me and lowered her head.

"Hey. Hey. Whatever it is, I got you. I got you," she whispered.

I nodded and began telling my story.

CHAPTER NINETEEN
EMMA
Three months earlier

The kitchen was trashed with plastic cups and used paper towels scattered everywhere. A tower of pizza boxes tilted on the table, sending the aroma of sausages, bacon, and various other types of meat floating in the air.

I stepped inside, breaking the sticky floor's grip on the soles of my shoes. The music blared from the other room, and people laughed while sipping their drinks.

"Save some for the rest of the party, Piggy."

I turned. Joshua was filling his cheeks with air and positioning his body, as if suddenly inflated. The guys around him chuckled, nudging each other and sharing high fives and fist bumps.

My eyes fell on Amy as her fingers curled around a slice of pizza, which dangled from her open mouth. Her eyes stared at Joshua and the guys, her cheeks red. She lowered her head and slid the pizza back onto her plate.

"Oink, oink," Joshua joked.

Amy scrambled to her feet and rushed out of the kitchen, knocking two guys aside.

"Earthquake," one said, waving his arms in an exaggerated state.

I shook my head.

"Jerks," I mumbled.

When I turned back, Michael had just walked over, carrying two red Solo cups.

"Where did these come from?" I asked.

He motioned to the counter, where a large punch bowl was sitting. Oh, party punch.

Since most of us were too young to buy alcohol, we often swiped whatever was around our houses. Then we'd bring it to the party, pour it into a large punch bowl, and let the party begin.

Oh, and for the record, by "we," I meant all the other people. I was far from a party person. My idea of parties was discussing the latest *Throne of Glass* novel in a book club that met every Wednesday at the library.

Michael had convinced me to come, and I only agreed to come tonight because Zahra was out visiting family for the weekend. I would do anything for Michael; sadly, I think he knew that.

I grabbed the cup and stared inside. A strange purplish-orange substance stared back at me. I didn't have the heart to ask what was in it.

Michael lifted his cup.

"Here's to... uh... finally being in the in-crowd," he said.

My chest tightened at the thought of this being his true desire, knowing it would probably end in heartbreak and pain.

82

It always did. The more he tried, the more ostracized he became to everyone else. I twisted my face but lifted my cup and tapped it against his.

"To being in the in-crowd."

I swallowed as the burning sensation slid down my throat, finding refuge in the pit of my stomach. I twisted my face, shaking the horrible taste out of my mind.

"I think I'm done after this one. I'm not made for this," I said, waving my hand in front of my face after another sip.

Michael laughed.

"No worries. One is all we need tonight. Let's go check out the D.J."

I nodded, and we proceeded to the living room. Drake's "God's Plan" slowly faded out, dissolving into Meek Mill's "I'm a Boss." The beautifully blended song blared through the giant speakers, rattling the walls, causing several picture frames to fall to the floor.

We found a place against the wall with a good view of the dance floor.

"Can you believe we were invited? I told you. One party, and we're in," he shouted.

"What?" I said.

"I said...," he paused, then shook it off as if it wasn't important.

The cup went to his lips, and his head tipped back.

"Hey, maybe you should slow down. We should maybe pace ourselves, right?" I said, leaning into his ear.

"I'm good."

The smile on his face was epic. I had never seen him so happy. His eyes scanned the room, jumping from one person to another. They finally settled on one person: Madison.

"I think I'm going to go talk to her. Should I go talk to her?" he said, glancing at her.

I shook my head, sighing heavily into my cup. I could feel the corners of my eyes becoming frozen with my tears. I turned away, wiping them quickly. Despite everyone in the room, I suddenly felt a million miles away, watching everyone else from the outside.

I turned back to Michael, but his body was already in motion before I could speak.

"I'll be back," he said over his shoulder.

I stared at the back of his head, wanting desperately to chase after him, and confess everything to him. Tell him I wanted him, with every fault, with every insecurity, everything. He was enough for me. He was always enough for me. But instead, my body froze, chilled by immobility.

I glanced around and slowly backed myself against the wall. It felt like the only safe place, the only place where I thought I belonged. I took another sip and then another.

After my cup was empty, my night only existed in flashes of time. And when the moments of memory did reappear, they were often hazy and filled with uncertainty about truths and things I just made up to fill in the gaps.

Things I remembered:

The music was still blasting, crumbling my eardrums.

My body being pushed as others bumped into me on the dance floor.

Stepping on someone's shoe and repeatedly apologizing.

Searching for Michael, but not finding him.

Slowly making my way to the kitchen table. I leaned on my arm as someone said I looked wasted.

Another cup was suddenly in front of me, while someone gently helped lift the cup to my mouth.

Fingers intertwining with mine. My legs felt sluggish as I tried to ascend the stairs.

A dark room. The only light source was the shine of the moon seeping into the room through the blinds.

Lips pressing against mine.

My hands pushing away as my pants loosened.

Michael's face looming over me. His eyes scanning mine, and me whispering, "I love you."

When I awoke, my heart sprinted from within as the

world screamed for my attention. Birds chirped like roaring dragons, while the heater boomed through the walls. The clicking of the clock pulsated throughout the room, and spotlights beamed into my soul as the sun peeked from the window. My eyes forced themselves shut at the brightness.

"What happened?" I asked, gripping my head with both hands. "Oh, my head..."

"Sorry, I didn't realize," a soft voice said.

I looked up to find Amy closing the window blinds.

"Where are we?" I asked.

"My bedroom."

I scanned the room with narrowed eyes. It reminded me of a bedroom you'd see in one of those sitcoms. The walls had posters of musical groups—Fall Out Boy hung next to Dropkick Murphy, while Eminem rested in the corner.

Two large bookshelves flanked her twin-size bed, covered in a pink throw blanket and gray sheets. Empty candy wrappers were sprayed across the floor, covering opened books and magazines about diets and healthy living. Talk about irony.

"Sorry, my place is a mess. I didn't expect... I mean, I didn't think..." Her rambling came to an end with a shrug of her shoulders.

"Why am I here? How did I get here?" I asked. The stench of my breath mortified me, but I couldn't do much to avoid it right now.

"I brought you here from the party," she said.

"Why?"

By this time, I had managed to sit up. I tried to focus on Amy, but balancing the spinning room was a challenge.

She didn't speak. She stared at me as she shifted in her seat. Her lips opened, but nothing came out.

"What is it?" I asked, confused about her paralyzed state.

"I found you at the party," she said flatly. "You were, uh... upstairs and pretty wasted."

"Wasted? I only had one drink," I said, recalling the previous night.

"Oh. Okay. Well, um," she stuttered.

"Amy."

Her head popped up and she stared at me.

"Just tell me why you brought me home," I command-ed.

She sighed and nodded.

"Okay. Okay. I found you upstairs. I had snuck to the bathroom upstairs, and when I came out, that guy you're always with was leaning over you. But it wasn't like in a friendly way, you know? I didn't think you wanted to be there. It just felt like something was off," she said, fidgeting.

"Michael? Wait..." I paused as the realization of her words finally sank in. "Are you saying he was..."

"I don't know. That's what it looked like. I mean, your pants were slid down, but you weren't awake, so I just figured..."

Amy sat there staring at the floor. My mind raced with questions. I did remember Michael staring at me. I remembered his eyes, his face. Oh, God.

My breath caught as flashes of memory drowned my thoughts. He did try to get me drunk, but he would never... would he? He wanted to be at the party so badly; would he do anything to keep appearances? No. I loved Michael and I would have given myself to him. There was no way he would. I shook the thought away, but something deep inside me grabbed the doubts and held on. Would he?

"There's no way," I said. "None at all. Maybe you just misinterpreted something." I pinched my lips for a moment. "Maybe you..."

"Your pants were unzipped, but you were beyond passed out. I didn't misinterpret it." Her tone turned harsh. "I know what I saw. I know."

I stared at her and saw pain reflecting back at me. I slowly nodded as sadness rushed through me. She jerked her head away, but tears were clearly forming.

I swallowed and said, "I should go. I have to go."

"You can stay. I can make breakfast or something," she said.

I stood up, throwing the blanket to the side.

"Wait," she said. "I mean, please."

I held my head down. I wanted to run. I wanted to scream. I wanted to... heck, I didn't know what I wanted to do, but I felt as if every inch of me was dirty like my skin wasn't my own. My brain stumbled into flashes of foreign fingers roaming across my body, stealing every part of me. I just wanted to go home and scrub myself clean. Scrub all of this nightmare away.

"Please." Her words were soft, pleading.

I looked up at her and thought maybe she needed me like I needed her. I nodded and sat back down.

CHAPTER TWENTY
EMMA

When I was done, I crumbled into Zahra's arms again, and all the sadness, shame, disgust, and anger I held inside finally rushed to the surface. My body grew weak, and my legs wobbled beneath me. Zahra lowered me to the curb and sat next to me, rubbing my back. The gentle breeze lifted strands of my hair, partially obscuring my vision.

We sat there for minutes, sharing each other's tears and pain.

"I'm sorry..." I began.

"No, don't do that. You have nothing to be sorry about," she said.

"But I should have done something. I should have been smarter or something. I should have..."

"Stop it. This isn't on you, and I refuse to let you blame yourself. This is that jerk Michael's fault."

Her head shook violently.

"Oh, my God." Her eyes went wide as she stared into the distance.

"What? What's wrong?"

"Michael." She turned back to me. "He's the one who convinced me to come. Oh my God. I'm about to..." She raised her fist, and her anger left her speechless.

I sniffed, wiping my nose with a Kleenex I grabbed from my pocket.

"I'm going to kill him. I'm so sorry, Em. I had no idea. I would have never suggested we come here. Let's go home. Forget this stupid party," she said.

"No," I said.

"No?"

"Yeah, no! I can't be a slave to fear for the rest of my life. I can't let him win," I said, straightening my posture. "Right?"

I turned to Zahra and watched her as she studied my face. She thought for a moment, silent as the night. Then she slowly nodded, and a smile appeared.

"Right, Azizam."

My jaw tightened, and heat flushed throughout my body.

"Right," I said. "We'll give it at least five minutes. If I feel uncomfortable, we'll leave after that. Banana split?"

"Banana split," Zahra said.

Banana split was our code word. Whenever we were somewhere and felt uncomfortable or just wanted to leave, we'd say "banana split." We had several other code words too; "black box" meant "I have a secret, but you can't tell anyone," and "tube socks" meant "he or she is cute, and you should go so I can handle my business." Zahra was always telling me the last code. Maybe one day I'd use it too.

I took a breath and said, "Five minutes."

A smile crossed her face, and she wrapped her arm around me again. With a few wipes of our tear-filled faces, we began walking.

"Did someone order Chinese food? I thought we were only having pizza," a familiar voice said as we walked up the driveway.

We turned to find Madison staring at us, with her nose scrunched up.

"Oh, Lucy Liu, I didn't recognize you," she said. Priscilla and Joshua giggled behind her.

"Madison," Michael said in a disapproving tone.

"What? Oh, come on, she looks just like that guy that delivers the Chinese food at my house."

"The guy?" I thought.

"And I see you brought a friend. Daddy let you out tonight?" she said.

Zahra and I shared confused looks, as did the others.

"What? Oh, come on. Am I the only one who notices the fingerprints on her arms? Look, if you ever feel unsafe, there are resources for abused children." Her voice was as condescending as her face.

Zahra crossed her arms, concealing the bruises. I swallowed, knowing the secrets she held. Secrets she wished were only visible within the walls of her house.

"Madison, that's messed up," Joshua said, but he sucked at hiding his laughter.

"Whatever," she said, turning away and heading inside. "I'm getting a drink."

"Jendeh," Zahra mumbled under her breath. She didn't need to translate that one for me to understand.

"Maybe we shouldn't..." Zahra began.

"Oh, banana split with whipped cream and a cherry on top," I whispered in her ear.

She giggled and nodded.

Michael's eyes fell upon mine. I looked at him but quickly glanced away. A hint of nausea rushed over me, and my body tightened.

"Hey," Michael said, his voice cracked. I stretched my lips out, forcing a fake smile.

"What's up, Zahra?" Joshua said, eyeing her up and down. His eyes paused a little too long at her chest, but he quickly recovered and managed to look into her eyes... eventually.

"Not your IQ, apparently," she joked.

His lips pinched, and he rolled his eyes.

"Let's go inside, babe," Priscilla said, grabbing Joshua's arm. Her eyes burned through Zahra as she lifted something to her lips.

She exhaled a giant translucent fog from her mouth that floated to us. A mixture of strawberry and beer wafted in the air, hitting me like a ton of bricks. I wrinkled my nose.

I never understood the fascination with vaping. I didn't mind if people did it, but I hated how it smelled. My stomach churned a bit.

Zahra smirked at Priscilla, who countered by rolling her eyes. I slowly stepped back, taking in the scene.

Overgrown weeds paraded the sides of the driveway, roaming through the cracks. An old basketball hoop stood at the side, and a tattered net barely clung on. Dark stains were soaked into the cracked cement.

The garage was enormous, with enough room for two cars. Inside, there was an assortment of items. Joshua's sporting equipment was shoved in an opened cabinet, with balls and bats spilling out.

A dartboard hung on the wall next to several punctured shooting range targets. A large gun safe sat securely in the corner. My eyes drifted to the far wall.

It looked like a museum of military equipment. Military insignia and older photos sat perched on the shelves. A folded American flag was laid in a triangular box, with a large black and white hat on top. Other military equipment and uniforms were tucked on the bottom shelf. Maybe the military was in his bloodline.

I stared at the camping gear when an intense feeling of being watched crept over me. From the corner of my eyes, I spotted a slim figure lurking in the shadows. His eyes wore a cloak of grief as they locked onto mine, drawing me towards him. But when I turned back to see if anyone else noticed him, no one seemed to realize his presence, just like the older woman in P.E. class.

My fingers tingled as something inside me drew me to the mysterious figure. I stepped forward, letting the others continue their conversation. As I approached, I reached out, but it vanished between blinks.

"Hey, what are you doing?" Joshua said.

I turned back to the group. Their eyes set upon me, and I opened my mouth to speak, but nothing came out.

Instead, a heaviness grew inside my chest, and my heart sunk into my stomach. The tingling ravaged my body, while darkness fell upon me, and my knees buckled. I looked up, but the group was gone.

CHAPTER TWENTY-ONE

EMMA

When I awoke, the party scene was no more, replaced by the stillness of the night. A pungent cloud of cigarette smoke wafted in the air, making my insides cringe with disgust.

Panic rushed over me as I realized I was no longer in control of my own body. My body stood immobile, disconnected from my senses. I screamed, but my words only echoed in another's mind. This wasn't like the forest. This was different.

My eyes, I mean, his eyes peered down at his hands, and my heart raced at the sight. Discolored red patches seeped into flaky, blistered material that used to be skin. His fingers floated to his lips as I felt a burning sensation rummage through his body.

He momentarily closed his eyes, trapping me in the darkness, until he finally released a smoky haze into the night's sky. I recoiled at the taste of the cigarette against his tongue. A warm beer rushed down his throat, and I fought the urge to gag.

After placing the bottle on the floor, he rummaged through his pocket and pulled out his phone. The top was cracked, but it still appeared to function correctly. His thumb slid across the fractured screen, stopping on a conversation he had with someone named Meredith. Seeing the name tightened my chest. He loved her. No, it was more than that. I could feel it.

His eyes stared at the message, allowing me a glimpse into his world.

"I can't do this anymore," she wrote.

"Do what?" he replied.

"You aren't the same guy you were. You're different. I'm sorry, but it's over," she said, followed by several sad face emojis.

His chest tightened, and I suddenly felt a stabbing sensation in my heart. The pain was intense, and a tsunami of sadness heightened it.

These were his emotions, but they rushed over me, drowning me inside him. I felt like I wasn't good enough, as if nothing was going right. I felt worthless. I could feel it all.

The heartbreak after being told I might never serve again. The failure in my parents' eyes every time they saw me. The countless rejections from companies saying I'm just not qualified enough. I served three years for a grateful nation, but I couldn't come home and get a freaking job. I felt my heart sink into my stomach.

He opened his email application, thumbing to an email from "Gunney."

"Devil Dogs, I just got word Lance Corporal didn't make it. They couldn't save him. I'm praying for him, his family, and you. Signed GySgt Ramirez."

He shook his head as a tear roamed down his cheek. More sadness crept into his soul—more drowning.

He flicked the cigarette stub, sending it shooting to the ground. He stood and stared out into the street.

The night was quiet and peaceful. There were no stars, no clouds, just a lonesome moon. The trees didn't even rustle because there was no wind—just complete and utter stillness.

He adjusted the chair, ensuring it was in the correct spot. Then, once satisfied, he adjusted his black Marine Corps uniform, ensuring it looked sharp. After a set of deep breaths, a strange tranquility fell upon us. A dark, heavy sense of relief coursed through him, as if he became lighter and his breathing eased.

Was he over the pain? Did he need a moment of calmness to ease his problems? My answers soon came when he stepped onto the chair.

He ducked his head inside the tied noose and pulled the top of the rope. He opened his mouth, and his gruff, deep voice emerged through the silence.

"From the Halls of Montezuma to the shores of Tripoli. We fight our country's battles in the air, on land, and...."

"No," I screamed, but my words echoed in my subconscious. "No, don't!"

We stepped off the chair, and time ceased to exist. His body jolted forward. Pressure tightened around his neck. Breathing became impossible. The salt of his tears seeped into the corners of his mouth. The bitterness of the alcohol lingered against his lips. His eyes bulged as our vision grew dark, until we were no longer we.

My eyes shot open, flooding every nerve in my body with pain and sadness. It was too much. My body crumbled to the ground as tears flowed like autumn rain. My fist flew to my chest, clutching it as if I feared my heart would explode with my next breath.

Zahra was by my side before I knew what hit me. Oh, Zahra. Seeing her brought some relief. I was back, no longer trapped within another's mind.

"Girl, you, okay? Emma?" she said, concern drowning in her voice.

My lips pursed as I exhaled a long, shaky breath. Then another. The world slowly reappeared as my eyes opened once again. I took in the scene.

Zahra was crouched next to me, her eyes blanketing me with worry. The others stood behind her. They all stared at me, sharing snickering whispers.

"Yeah. I'm okay," I said. I slid my hands into hers and squeezed. "I'm fine."

"Girl, are you okay?" Zahra asked again, scanning my body for any cuts or bruises.

"Yeah." I shook my head and stood up. "I felt so sad. It was crushing."

"Wait, the superpower?"

I nodded.

"Well, you're okay now," she said, touching my shoulder. Her multiple-colored bracelets jingled with every movement.

"Yeah," I said, taking another deep breath.

"What the hell was that?" Priscilla asked.

"That was freaking crazy," Michael said in a hushed tone.

"Who are you calling crazy?" Zahra turned. I had to hold her back to prevent her from punching the boy.

"Oh," Priscilla said, "you 'bout to get your butt whooped, Michael."

Zahra brushed my grip off and stormed towards him.

"You call my girl crazy one more time," she said, stabbing him in the chest with her fingers, "I'll definitely lay the smackdown."

Michael's face turned pale as he backpedaled.

"No, I didn't say she was…," he began.

"We'll see how you like it when someone puts their hands on you without permission, little boy," she interrupted.

"Lay the smackdown?" Priscilla snickered.

Joshua stood and cocked his head. His eyes were wide, focusing directly on me.

I stepped to Zahra, and she intertwined her arm with mine as we strolled off, leaving the guys behind us.

"But I didn't say she was crazy. I said it was crazy," Michael said, but his voice faded as our distance grew.

CHAPTER TWENTY-TWO

EMMA

"Well, we have to watch the public shows of your weird superpower," Zahra said, reaching for two solo cups.

"It's not my fault, and it's not a superpower, more like a curse," I said.

"I really think we need to figure this thing out. You could be the next Wonder Woman," she said, handing me a cup.

"Let's say we go that route and I become a superhero," I began.

"Yes," she said excitedly.

"With ever superhero there is," I paused.

"Dang. A supervillain. Good point," she said looking defeated.

I slowly sipped the drink, not thinking about my actions, and instantly regretted it.

"What the hell is this?"

"No clue. It was just in the punch bowl. Based on the look of it," she leaned into the purplish-green mixture, "and the smell of it, I'm sure it's 100 percent toxic."

"Oh great. First, I'll die of embarrassment, and then I'll die of poison. Makes sense," I said.

I placed the cup on the counter and stepped back. The aftertaste lingered in my mouth, making my taste buds scream for mercy. I paused, realizing this was the first drink I'd had since...

"It can't be that bad." Zahra lifted her cup and took a sip. She flinched, coughing into her elbow. "I was wrong," she said in an unsteady voice, "so wrong."

With new cups filled only with water, we headed into the living room, where the party was all the way up. The volume boomed from the gigantic speakers as the DJ merged two songs into one beautiful melody, mixing Eminem's vocals on a Jackson Five beat. It was unexpected, but it went well together.

We squeezed behind a couple, making out; her tongue was so deep in his throat, I'm sure she could tell what he had for dinner... three weeks ago. Next to them stood a slender guy with shoulder-length, unkempt hair. His smudged glasses teetered off his nose as he snuck glances at the couple as if this night couldn't get any weirder.

I nudged Zahra, pointing to the nerds. "And this is why I don't do parties."

She laughed and leaned in. "Say the word, and I'll hook you up. I think you both need a little practice." I pushed her shoulder, making her accidentally spill her drink.

After scanning the room for a bit, we finally found a seat on the couch, sharing it with a girl taking selfies. She'd take the picture, review it, and then try it again. This went on for longer than it should have.

With a few mixes of the record, J.Cole's voice blasted through the speakers, sending people to the makeshift dance floor. Even Zahra and I bobbed to the beat and recited the lyrics. It felt good to let loose and have fun, but at the same time, a little piece of me was still guarded.

Surprisingly, even Madison was on the dance floor. I didn't think she was into hip-hop.

As the music boomed, everyone screamed the lyrics, bodies gyrating and arms flying through the air. Then, a part of the song roared through the speakers where the artist used the n-word. First of all, there were three people of color here: Zahra, me, and Stanley Rodrick Banks, better known as DJ Panda Bear, meaning the DJ. Yep, three people here were not white, well, entirely white.

Most people wouldn't use the word when repeating the lyrics. This wasn't a rule found in schoolbooks or libraries, but just one of those unspoken rules. Not here.

DJ Panda Bear must have been looking out in the crowd because he noticed one person shouting the very offensive word as the song played. Most people would ignore it, but DJ Panda Bear was a DJ, so with a few twists of his fingers, the song replayed moments before that line boomed through the speakers. And when the line played, the crafty DJ Panda Bear lowered the volume so all you heard was one voice shouting the n-word at the top of her lungs.

The music stopped, and everyone turned to Madison. Her dancing ceased, and she turned surprised.

"What happened to the music?" she asked.

Priscilla leaned in and whispered something to her. I couldn't tell what it was, but Madison erupted, "If they didn't want us to say it, why put it in their songs? White people are the number one buyers of rap music. Look it up. It just makes sense that they want us to say it. Plus, it's a song, people. Get over it."

The partygoers glanced back at one another with hushed whispers.

"Play the music," Madison yelled. "Play. The. Music," she yelled breaking down every syllable.

Zahra turned to me and smiled. I gave her a guilty smile as we waited for Madison to lower her head in shame. But to our surprise, Madison's yells were soon joined by Priscilla's, then a few more kids, until the entire room demanded DJ Panda Bear continue playing.

Something inside of me broke at this reality. DJ Panda Bear recoiled at the chants, mouthing the words, "Are you serious?" He shook his head, shooting his empty palms in the air.

"Play the music," the chants continued.

He took off his headphones, placing them on the turntable. Was he really packing up? Zahra and I shared concerned glances as more chants erupted from the crowd.

"Play. The. Music."

DJ Panda Bear's hand hung over his equipment as he closed his eyes. His head twisted as if having an internal battle with himself. Moments later, his eyes reappeared, and he adjusted his headphones over his ears, taking a deep, slow breath. With a few taps to his equipment, the music once again blared out of the speakers, sending people back into their party state.

"What the hell?" Zahra said. "Why did he put the music back on?"

I didn't even bother with a response. I just shook my head. I wasn't surprised. How could I be? I knew Madison and I knew her ability to change individuals into cowards she could control. Madison for the win, again.

After a few moments, Zahra spoke.

"How's the living situation going?" she asked.

"It's going. It's like a funeral home now, it's so quiet," I said. "It's hard, ya know, because of Mom and," I sighed, "I don't know. It's just hard."

"Yeah, I bet," she said, sharing a pained glance.

"How about you?" I asked.

A guy barreled through us, spilling his drink on my shoe.

"Hey," Zahra screamed but the guy was already stumbling out the door. "It's going," she said.

We both stared at the partygoers, seeking a distraction from our home lives. Our eyes turned to a girl from my English class— Becky, I think, no Betsy— who tried and failed to do a sensual dance while hovering over her boyfriend. As her skirt slid up, his face morphed into a giant leering grin, like a jack-o-lantern.

On the far wall, a big guy passed a little plastic baggy to a set of blondes. They examined the bag, nodded their approval, and dashed to the kitchen, hoping to elevate the party a bit. I shook my head.

"Cheers," Zahra said, holding her cup up to me.

I raised my cup.

"Cheers."

As the music continued, Zahra and I watched in amusement. Suddenly, the cold feeling of eyes peering into my soul emerged from a few feet away. It was Joshua.

His eyebrows furrowed as his blue eyes shot daggers in my direction.

"Uh, are you seeing this too?" Zahra asked.

"Yeah, he looks pissed."

Joshua raised his solo cup and took a sip, never breaking eye contact with me.

"Did I do something wrong?" I whispered to Zahra.

"I don't think so. Maybe..."

"You think it's cool to make fun of my brother?"

His words flew at me, slicing the fun and laughter of the crowd in half. More eyes turned in our direction.

Zahra and I shared confused looks. Joshua's eyebrows furrowed, face reddened. Michael, who magically appeared behind Joshua, stood there shocked. His smile quickly faded as he no doubt saw the confusion and fear in our eyes.

"You think that's funny? You think that crap is funny, huh?" Joshua roared.

At this time, Zahra and I were on our feet.

"What?" I stuttered. "What did I do?"

Joshua stepped forward, and we inched backward. Unfortunately, the couch limited our spacing. The music suddenly went silent as the entire party admired the show. At least if he tried to kill us, there'd be witnesses.

"Oh, don't even act like you don't know." Joshua took another step closer.

Michael reached out his hand again, gripping Joshua's forearm.

"Bro, maybe you should cool it. This isn't funny, man. Maybe we should..." Michael began.

Joshua jerked his arm away, but thankfully, he didn't press forward. Instead, his jaw tightened, sending veins throbbing throughout his neck.

I could feel Zahra's fingers wrap around mine.

"Fine," Joshua began. "Get the hell out."

"Joshua, we didn't do anything to you or your brother," Zahra protested.

"Get out of my house, now," he commanded. His eyes now honed in on her.

"This is some..." Before Zahra could continue, I raised my hand, silencing her mid-sentence. Joshua turned back to me.

"We'll go, Joshua. But we didn't do anything to your brother, and we definitely weren't making fun of him," I said. My voice was gentler than I expected.

I stared into his eyes for a moment, hoping to find some gleam of light, hoping that a small part of him believed me. Wait, his eyes.

His eyes threw me back to being in the driveway. While Priscilla was joking around, and Michael was busy calling people crazy, Joshua stood there, frozen in time. His reaction after I came to wasn't what it appeared.

His eyes were wide, drowning his ocean eyes in a sea of white. His jaw was slightly ajar. He wasn't laughing; he was shocked.

"Whatever," Zahra said, interrupting my attempts to reconstruct the pieces in my head. She stepped around the couch and headed to the door.

I followed and then stopped. I turned back to Joshua. He didn't have to say what happened to his brother. I already knew. When I collapsed outside in the driveway, I saw it all.

I wanted to run to him and hug him tightly, letting him know I knew what he was going through. I wanted to tell him I truly understood the horrors of his brother's death. But I couldn't. There was no way in this world he would understand. So, I turned and walked out the door.

CHAPTER TWENTY-THREE

EMMA

Zahra quietly opened the door, and we both stepped in. The smell of dinner from that night lingered in the air while the television glowed, illustrating the dark room.

Her dad was sprawled across the couch, the remote barely hanging from his fingertips. He wore his work clothes, with the tie loosely draped around his neck.

Zahra walked over slowly and covered him with a throw blanket. He stirred but didn't wake. After switching off the television, our attention turned to noises from the kitchen.

"Oh no," she mumbled as she headed around the corner.

"What's going..." My words trailed off as I saw what had captured her attention.

Her mom stood in the kitchen, sweeping, her movements synchronized with an imaginary song playing only for her.

"Mama," Zahra said gently, "what are you doing?"

Her mom paused and looked up. Her gaze froze for a moment before she suddenly snapped out of it.

"Just cleaning the floor, Azizam. This place is so filthy. I'll never get it clean before Greg's parents arrive."

Zahra glanced at me and nervously bit her bottom lip.

"Emma, how are you, dear?" her mom asked, briefly interrupting her cleaning.

"Hey, Mama Parviz," I replied.

"Please tell your mom I'll bring her a piece of my peach cobbler tomorrow. Unless that one over there," she motioned towards Zahra, "eats it first." Her face lit up with a smile.

"Mama," Zahra scolded. "Okay, let's go to bed, Mama. You can sweep tomorrow." Zahra gently took her mom's hand, snatching the broom away.

"But Azizam, there's no need to be rude," her mom protested.

Zahra huffed. "I'm not trying to be rude, Mama. It's just really late. It's past midnight. Let's get you to bed."

Her tone softened, which seemed to work better with her mom.

Mama Parviz smiled and nodded her head. She shuffled past me and stopped. Touching my shoulder, she whispered, "Make sure you tell your mom about that cobbler now, okay?"

"That's enough, Mama," Zahra grimaced. "Let's go," she said, gently leading her mom down the hall.

I sat on a stool, my eyes wandering around the kitchen. The refrigerator was adorned with magnets representing different states. A peach-shaped magnet hung beside a sunglasses-wearing flamingo, and a large outline of California kissed the Texas-shaped magnet.

A faint smell of burning reached my nose. Turning to the stove, I noticed a pan sitting atop high flames. Smoke whiffed from the pan.

"No, no, no," I gasped, dashing toward the stove.

I reached for the pot, only to be greeted by a sharp, intense pain shooting through my hand. Flinching backward, I dropped the pot and a loud bang reverberated throughout the house.

"What's going on?" Zahra asked, rushing around the corner.

I extended my hand, trying to ease the burning sensation.

"Not again," she muttered. "I can't stand her."

"Another bad day?" I asked.

Zahra leaned against the counter, hiding her face in her hands.

"Sorry about her asking about your mom and stuff. She's just..." Her voice trailed off as if unable to finish her thought.

"It's not a big deal she asked," I assured her. "They have been friends almost as long as us."

Zahra nodded while unpeeling her face from her hands.

"She seems so different," I acknowledged.

Memories of who Mama Parviz used to be flooded my mind. It was her zest for life and adventure that drew me into her like a moth to a flame. She was like the fun aunt everyone wanted. That was probably why we turned to her when the other parents wouldn't let us get our way.

Late-night movie marathons were our secret rebellion. She'd let us stay up late watching scary movies; our favorite was a Korean zombie movie called *Train to Busan*. Mama Parviz would always sneak behind the couch before the first zombie attack. Then, she'd jump up, reaching out for us, unleashing a parade of screams and laughter that reverberated throughout the house. This happened every time we watched it, and of course, we always knew it was coming, but we didn't care. We played along because it was her.

Mama Parviz even took me to get my ears pierced, despite several objections from my parents. After it was done and the pain eventually subsided, I hid my ears under the veil of my long hair for two weeks before anyone noticed.

When my parents did find out, my mom marched to Zahra's house, mumbling every Hmong curse word under her breath, determined to tell Mama Parviz off. Ironically, that confrontation launched the two into a beautiful relationship that blossomed into a sisterhood that still remains strong. Mom and Mama Parviz never told us what happened. But we had our theories.

I thought Mom stormed over, but when Mama Parviz opened the door, her tough exterior morphed into the sweet woman I was used to. After that, the two had a calm, respectful conversation and made up, instant friends.

Zahra had a different take. She thought Mom stormed over and the two had an epic battle, *Kill Bill* style. After the bloodshed and choice words exchanged, the two realized they would be better as partners than enemies. And so began the unlikely duo of Mom and Mama Parviz. Since we didn't really know the truth, we agreed to disagree.

My heart lit up at the thought of Mama Parviz. She was something special. But for the past few months, she hadn't been the same. Everything had changed. It was as if she had forgotten how to be herself.

Sometimes, her mood would change in a flash, causing her to go into a deep anger. I glanced down at the purple blotches on Zahra's arms, and think back to the one night, I came over and Mama Parviz had thrown pots and pans at Mr. Greg, Zahra's dad. We tried to calm her, but the only remedy was time. This was before we knew she was sick, before any of us knew how to care for her.

"Sorry about Joshua. He's such a jerk," Zahra said, changing the subject.

"Actually, I deserved it," I said, sitting back on the stool.

She looked at me, her eyebrows furrowed.

"How in the world do you deserve it?"

Zahra grabbed a bag of Oreos and slid them in front of me.

"I saw it. I saw his brother. You know, like before, like the old lady."

"Wait. Like your superpower?" she gasped, nearly choking on her cookie.

"It was crazy. It wasn't like before. I've never felt that way about someone," I said.

"How so?"

"Joshua's brother was so sad, even worse than sad." I paused and stared as I spun the cookie on the counter. Thoughts of his emotions crept back, but I refused to delve into them again, once was enough.

I explained what I saw, keeping true to every detail, no matter how big or small. Her face slacked as I recalled the messages from Gunney and the breakup, and her lips trembled at the vivid imagery of stepping off the chair. Even retelling it was just too much.

I had never been suicidal, but I almost drowned in his pool of pain and hopelessness. Just living through it left me drained.

I flinched as Zahra placed her hand on my shoulder.

"Hey," she said, lowering her head to meet my eyes. "You're not him anymore. You're not him."

I nodded but couldn't hold back the tears. My hands trembled as I took a deep breath. She wrapped me in her arms, enveloping me with her love.

CHAPTER TWENTY-FOUR

EMMA

I spent the night at Zahra's house and walked home early the following day. Luckily, she only lived down the street, a quick trip. Usually, my parents wouldn't let me walk alone at night, but early mornings were considered pretty safe. Most of the "criminals," as my dad put it, were already sleeping off their highs or drowning in their lows.

When I walked in, my parents were sitting at the table. You know that feeling when you walk into a room, and everyone suddenly goes quiet? Well, this wasn't like that. There was already silence before I even stepped inside.

The light of the new day's sun kissed the side of my mom's face, highlighting her deep, warm skin as she stood by the window. Her eyes searched for something that wasn't there and she remained lost in her own thoughts. For a second, Mama Parviz floated in my mind. Mom glanced over at me momentarily but then retreated to the window.

My dad quickly stood and reached for his belongings.

"Hey, glad I caught you. I'm working a double tonight, so…"

"You're working another double? Again?"

He paused, examining me.

"Whatever, it's fine," I frowned.

"So, make sure you take the trash out," he said, reaching for the keys.

"Yes sir," I mumbled.

"Don't forget the cemetery on Saturday. I would love to have you there. Think it'd be good for your mom, too. I think she really, really needs that and," he paused, "I think it would bring you peace as well."

I turned to her, but she didn't budge. Dad leaned in, hugged me, and then hurried out the door.

The sound of keys rattling from the other side of the door quickly faded, replaced by a hushed atmosphere. After a few moments, there was only silence.

My gaze turned away and I scanned the room. A half-eaten TV dinner sat on the table, waiting for Dad's return. Crumbs were scattered around the tray. The seat remained pushed away from the table. The kitchen was cluttered, with a pile of mail sprawled along the counter. The TV dinner box was balanced on the rim of the trash can.

I looked up to find my mom glancing over at me. She smiled and I returned the smile, but I felt like my heart was breaking from within.

The accident changed our dynamic. My mom hardly talked, and my dad, well, he worked nonstop now. I barely saw him anymore. He should be home, mending this fractured family, being our backbone. But he was working another double, again. Despite my anger towards him, I knew I couldn't hold it all against just him. Plus, I knew he blamed himself for the accident.

"Hey, Mom. Are you okay?" I asked.

She nodded, shooting me her angelic smile.

"Okay. I'm going to grab something to eat. I'm starving." I entered the kitchen, grabbed a bowl and cereal from the cupboard, and returned to the table.

As I crunched on the Frosted Cheerios, I could feel the warm sensation of eyes burying deep inside me.

You know how parents can give you that one look that means so much? The look that asks where you were last night, who you were with, and why didn't you come home earlier. Well, this was that look.

I could try to wait her out, but she had better patience than I did. I slammed the spoon into the bowl.

"Fine, I was out with Zahra. It was just a house party. I don't remember seeing any boys. No, I didn't do drugs and stayed at her house after it ended. Nothing happened."

I exhaled as if I had just revealed all my untold secrets to a foreign spy torturing me in a deep, dark dungeon. She turned and smiled, raising an eyebrow.

"And yes, I had fun," I said, returning her smile.

CHAPTER TWENTY-FIVE

MICHAEL

At lunch, I stepped into the cafeteria as the explosion of chatter and laughter welcomed me. The room was packed. People were talking with friends between bites of packed lunches and school-provided snacks. I slid through the narrow passage and joined Madison and the gang at the table at the far end of the cafeteria.

"About time. What were you doing by yourself? Flipping the bean?"

"I don't even know what that means," I said. I reached over, gave Priscilla a high five, and smiled at Madison. "What's going on?"

I slid my tray onto the table, spilling some of my water.

"Clutts," Joshua joked.

Priscilla handed me a few napkins, and I dabbed the stain.

"Okay," Priscilla said, continuing the conversation I had interrupted. "Have you heard this one? It's fire," she said, nodding while handing Joshua her left earbud.

He looked up as he listened. His head suddenly rocked to the beat, and a smile soon appeared.

"Yeah, I like this. We were rocking this at P.E."

Priscilla gently grabbed the earpiece from her boyfriend and offered it to me.

"Wanna listen? It's Jack Harlow. He's about to blow up."

I popped my head up from the pizza I was devouring and nodded. I leaned over the table and positioned the earbud. Priscilla leaned forward as well, allowing her headphones to reach both of us.

Priscilla glanced at me as we hovered above the center table, faces mere inches away. Her eyes moved from my eyes to my lips. Joshua was too busy folding his pizza in half and shoveling it in his mouth to notice.

I quickly looked down at the table and focused on the music. My head rocked up and down while the music splashed against my eardrums.

"This is cool," I said.

Her eyes moved to my mouth as a subtle grin stretched across her lips. I quickly ripped the earpiece out and sat back in my chair.

"Thanks," I mumbled.

"Anytime."

She gave me another smile as she sat back in her chair. I turned to Joshua, but he was oblivious to the flirtatious looks his girlfriend was giving me. Wait, was she flirting with me? Being on this side of it was somewhat new to me, but there was no way. Maybe she just liked to smile at people. That was it. She was a smiler. Right?

"I can't wait for summer. School is so boring now," Madison chimed in.

"You doing anything?" Priscilla asked.

"Maybe Paris or Spain again. That'd be cool. Anything foreign is good with me."

Madison stared at her fingers, rubbing each nail with her thumb.

"Well, I'll just be happy not to have to work. My parents are making me save up for a car," Priscilla said.

Madison grimaced. "What? Your parents are the worst," she snickered, not looking up from her nails.

Priscilla glanced down and laughed slightly, "Yeah, the worst." She rubbed the back of her head and then glanced over at me.

"Knowing my mom, I'd be lucky even to have enough for a bus ride," I joked.

Priscilla smiled. "Yeah."

"Whatever," Joshua began with what seemed like the entire slice of pizza in his mouth. "I'm glad I got a ride."

"Wasn't that your brother's car?" I asked.

Priscilla shot me a glare. Her lips squeezed tight, and she shook her head. Joshua's head lowered as he focused on his plate.

"We don't talk about his brother. I thought you, of all people, would know that," Madison said.

"What?" I looked over at Joshua. "Bro, my bad, man. I didn't mean…"

"Just shut up already, man. I don't care. It's whatever." He grabbed another slice, bent it in half, and shoved it in his mouth.

"No table manners," Madison said.

"What did you…" Joshua began but was quickly cut off by another voice.

"Oh, hey, Michael."

I looked over. Stanley was waving at me. He held his lunch tray with one hand and threw up two fingers.

"Hey," I said with a smile.

He glanced at Madison, and the two had a non-verbal battle with their eyes. A rosy glow fell upon Madison's cheeks as she swept Stanley away with her hands.

"Whatever," Stanley said, staring her down. "Alright, Michael, I'll catch you later."

Madison's eyes tightened as she watched him walk away.

"See, that's someone you should be mad at, Joshua," she said, pointing in Stanley's direction.

"Why would he be mad at him?" Priscilla asked.

"Are you serious?" Madison crossed her arms and leaned back. "He basically called me a racist at the party, which we all know I'm not. Most of Daddy's workers are foreign. Plus, I don't even see color."

I felt a throbbing in my chest as my eyes went wide.

"Yeah, and?" Joshua asked, reaching over and stealing one of Priscilla's pepperonis.

Madison rolled her eyes.

"Uh, if I'm a racist, which again I'm definitely not, that means you're a racist, by association. Get it? We hang out together. I bet he even put Emma up to make fun of your brother. Just like them to stick together."

"Them?" Priscilla questioned.

"Emma wasn't making fun of your brother; she must have…." I began.

"Oh, look who's talking—the same guy who just brought up Joshua's brother. Don't act like you didn't know that was a sensitive subject for Josh," Madison said, now pointing her finger at me.

"Joshua," Joshua corrected under his breath.

"But, I …I didn't know," I turned to Joshua, "I swear, man."

Joshua's hands balled into fists. The veins on his forehead bulged as his head lowered.

"Joshua? Don't do anything stupid," Priscilla warned. Her hand slid across his forearm. She ducked her head down to meet his eyes.

"Baby?"

But he was on his feet before we could even take another breath.

CHAPTER TWENTY-SIX

EMMA

"Guess who's the talk of the school again," Zahra said, squeezing beside me at the table. Her tray clattered against the table as she lowered her body next to mine.

"What? I'm trying to avoid being noticed."

"Well, you're not doing a great job of that," Zahra said. "And it doesn't help that this is a small town. No one has anything better to do than gossip."

She spun her tray around so her pizza was directly in front of her. She picked it up and took a bite, never taking her eyes off me. Steam rose from the piece as grease dripped onto her plate.

"What now?" I asked.

"The rumor is that you were making fun of Joshua's brother, the military hero and Red Heart recipient," she said.

"Purple Heart," I corrected, "and no, I didn't. You know that."

I grabbed my sandwich from my plate and crunched into it, causing the contents to slide out. I scooped up the tomato before it slid out and popped it into my mouth. BLTs were my absolute favorite, but the bacon had to be almost burnt, none of that soggy stuff.

"Well, it doesn't matter what I know," she said, picking a pepperoni from her plate.

"I need to figure this stuff out," I said, rubbing my hands with the napkin.

"What stuff? Oh, the superpower?" she asked.

"Okay, calm down. This isn't as interesting as you make it out to be," I said.

"Girl, yeah, it kinda is. Avengers, here we come, and then The Rock."

I put my hand up to gesture to lower her voice. The cafeteria was filled with the chatter of other students and the scraping of forks against their plates. Paper bags crumpled on my left as a kid finished the last of his lunch and tossed the bag in the trash. Despite all this, her excitement drew undue attention from the kids across from us. I was trying to stay under the radar, and she wasn't helping.

"Sorry," she said, adjusting her volume. "So, what are we going to do?"

"We?" I asked.

"Yeah, we're in this together."

I shook my head and took another bite of my sandwich as my mind retraced the memory.

"Creeper alert," she said, bumping my shoulder.

I looked up as she gestured across the cafeteria. One student was staring in our direction through the students enjoying their meatless lasagna and paper bag lunches. Michael.

"I'm about to go lay the smackdown," Zahra said, standing to her feet.

I grabbed her arm and pulled her down. Her body jerked down with a thud.

"Girl, you know I need that later. That's my best asset; you can't be breaking my butt like that," she said, rubbing her butt.

"First, definitely change the catchphrase. Second, sorry for you and your asset," I said, smiling. "But leave him alone. I want nothing to do with him and want to stay as far away as possible. For all I care, he doesn't exist."

"Well, for a guy who doesn't exist, he sure likes to stare."

I peered in Michael's direction and caught him stealing glances at me. I turned away and returned to my BLT, but thoughts of our past resurfaced.

It was only three months ago, our feet dangled from the rooftop as the sun painted a gorgeous orangish-purple glow over the city. Tiny goosebumps covered my arms as the autumn breeze flowed against my skin.

"I will never get used to this view," Michael said.

I turned and took him in. His eyes looked like the deepest of chocolates. His skin reminded me of honey. I stopped at his lips as he spoke. They were perfect. Not too thin, but not too thick either, and very kissable.

He turned.

"What do you think?" Michael asked.

My eyes jerked from his lips to his eyes as I scrambled to remember what he was talking about. Something about sports, no, perhaps the weather.

He sighed.

"Well, should I make my move?"

"Oh, yeah," I said. I bobbed my head as if I was seriously considering his question. I placed my hand on my chin as strands of hair swept along my cheek.

"What again?" I finally asked.

"Should I ask Madison to hang out?" His words were slow. "See, I knew you weren't listening," he said, smiling his sweet smile.

"What? I was listening." I placed my hand over my heart. "I am offended. I was definitely listening."

Michael rolled his eyes. The wind gently blew against him, pushing his shirt against his chest, another momentary distraction.

"Then should I hang with her or not?"

"No, she's the worst," I said quickly. "She's like the worst of the worst. The devil himself would cross the street if he saw her coming." I placed my hands on his shoulders and shook him. "And that's the devil."

He laughed as his head bobbled back and forth.

"But let's say she, Madison, not the devil," he began. I smiled and shook my head. He continued, "says we should hang, then we're officially part of the in-crowd. We'll go to parties..."

"I don't do parties," I said.

"Go to clubs...," he continued.

"Nope," I interrupted.

"Be popular."

I knew Michael better than anyone, and that was his deepest desire: to be popular, to fit in. He never listened when I told him that his insecurities wouldn't just vanish because people knew who he was. If anything, they probably got worse.

Plus, those insecurities were what made Michael Michael. His self-doubt made him sympathetic to others. His yearning to belong made him loyal beyond belief, because he cherished those around him that much more. And the shaggy hair, well, he just looked so cute.

He stopped and stared at me.

"What's so wrong with that?" he asked. "What's so wrong with Madison? She's cool. She's nice to us."

"Are you serious? She has picked on us our entire lives. I'm pretty sure the second I was born, and the doctor was about to slap my little bottom, Madison burst through the door and said 'no, let me do it' just so she could legally smack me, with no repercussions."

He shook his head but smiled.

"I really don't understand. Why do you need her to tell you you're cool? I tell you that every day. Do I not matter?" I asked.

He sighed.

"Of course, you matter. You're the most important person in my life…."

My heart exploded, and a sudden warmth flowed through me. The little butterflies in my stomach began a choreographed dance to my heartbeat.

"But of course, you're going to say I'm cool. You're like family. Family has to tell each other how great they are."

I imagined Leonardo from the Ninja Turtles sneaking onto the roof, tiptoeing behind me, stabbing me in the back, and slicing my heart into two.

The old "we're family" line. Maybe that was worse than "you're like my sister" because he didn't even specify that I was like his sister. Perhaps he saw me as that aunt who drank too much on holidays or that uncle no one let babysit.

"Does that make sense?" he said.

He stared into my eyes, and I saw the need to feel the love he so desired. I smiled because, in a way, I yearned for that same love. But I didn't need it from any other kids in our class. I needed it from him. He was my best friend, and it felt as if he was the only one who truly understood me. Just being around him made me feel somewhat whole.

I sighed. The butterflies in my stomach slowed until they were perfectly still.

"Yeah, I get it," I said.

"You know me. You know my life. I've been picked on since day one. If it wasn't the braces, it was the acne or my stupid hair…"

"I like your hair," I interrupted.

THE MASKS WE WEAR

"Or whatever. There's always something holding me back. I'm tired of being the punchline in everyone's joke. I want to tell the joke now."

I scrunched my face, and he mirrored my expression.

"You know what I mean," he said, flustered. "I want to go to parties and have girls interested in me."

Wow, that one stung a bit, but that was a secret best kept to myself.

"I want to be respected."

"I get it. I really do." I let out an exhaustive breath. "Fine, we can go to the stupid party. Happy?"

He extended a balled fist in my direction. I stared at it momentarily until I finally banged my fist against his.

"You'll see, once I'm in, you and Zahra will be next, and we'll be running this school," he said.

"Yeah," I said quietly.

I smiled, hoping he wouldn't see the insincerity on my face or hear the shakiness in my voice.

As usual, I put on my mask. A mask that said I was nothing more than just a friend. A mask I had been wearing for years, since the first moment I ever saw him. It was the only way I could keep him close to me. For once, I wished I had built up enough courage to tell him everything I felt. Maybe if I had told him, we wouldn't be in this mess. We'd be on his roof, holding hands, stealing kisses between laughs, and planning a future together. But I didn't tell him, because he made it perfectly clear. I wasn't the one he wanted.

Ding
Ding
Ding

A ringing bell interrupted my memory, and I stood and began collecting my belongings. Zahra and the rest of the cafeteria were still sitting when I looked around.

"Where are you going?" Zahra asked.

"The bell just rang."

"Uh, we still have like fifteen minutes," she said, looking down at her watch.

Her face twisted as she watched me lower to my chair. I could have sworn I heard a bell.

"Is this another superhero thing?"

I turned behind me and glanced through the cafeteria. Something was off.

"Emma?"

My eyes roamed through the students until I saw a small light shimmering in the background. I tilted my head and squeezed my eyes together.

"What is..." I began, but before I could finish, the light engulfed me in its existence. The chatter of the students was no more. The clanging of forks against trays disappeared, and all that was left was the light.

CHAPTER TWENTY-SEVEN

EMMA

The light dissipated, and everything was transformed. A low hum flowed throughout the room, replacing the vibrant sounds of the cafeteria. The sound of heavy wind crept in the background as orange flickers from lanterns while incense roamed through the crisp air. The entrance to the room was open, revealing a majestic sight. Snow blanketed the world, creating a wonderland effect. Snow-covered temples appeared in the background, in front of large mountain peaks. Colorful flags rippled in the wind, while snow flurries twisted and twirled.

It was weird. The coldness touched my skin, but all I felt was warmth, a warmth that floated all around me and inside me.

"What the hell?" I exclaimed.

I felt my heart racing as I took in the scene.

"Breathe," said a voice ringing in my ears. "Calm yourself, child."

I looked around, but there was no one in sight. After several moments, I finally realized the voice came from within me, or rather, inside the body I now possessed.

"Breathe," it said again.

My eyes peered down. Dark orange covered my body. My legs crossed as my fingers lay flat against my thighs.

"Breathe," he said. "Breath is life."

I stopped and focused my attention on the voice. My chest expanded and then slowly contracted.

"Life is breath, and breath is life," he said. He repeated that several times, but it wasn't to me. It was to himself. This body, this person, was speaking to himself, chanting to himself. That was why the humming was so vibrant; it was coming from him.

I sat in the stillness of the moment, taking in the scene, listening to his voice.

"Breathe."

My heart slowed. The heaviness of the moment slowly faded, and my soul relaxed.

"Breathe."

I closed my eyes and was taken away by the comfort of his voice. I felt everything in that moment, my lungs expanding, filling with the crisp air, then deflating. I felt my heart drum to life in a rhythmic manner.

"Breathe."

I felt the vibration of my lips as the humming came alive once more. Most importantly, I felt peace coursing through my soul, wrapping itself around me and pulling me into the light. It felt like the sun and the moon, like dark and light, all at the same time. It encased me in itself, and I loved it.

134

"Breathe."

The warmth soon faded. The peace soon ended and so did the silence of the moment. I was back in my world. I was back at school.

I turned to find Zahra and the rest of my table staring at me.

"What are you guys looking at?" Zahra barked. She turned to me and whispered, "Superpower?"

I nodded.

"Superpower."

"What happened?" she whispered.

I opened my mouth to speak, but the sound of oohs and ahhs erupted behind me. We both glanced over. Joshua was pounding away at another guy. Oh my gosh, it was Stanley— DJ Panda Bear.

Joshua's fists collided against Stanley's face, shooting blood onto the cement. Students gathered like vultures, waiting to feed their curiosity.

"Oh no," I said under my breath.

I didn't know Stanley that well, but no one deserved a beating like that. His head bounced off the cafeteria floor with every punch, sending a horrific thud echoing throughout the crowd.

Joshua's fist froze mid-air as his head lifted. His eyes went straight to Madison. A slow, menacing grin stretched along her face.

Suddenly, Michael stepped past her, but Madison quickly clenched his elbow as if she was preventing him from stopping all of this. Michael shook his head. Madison leaned into him and whispered something. I couldn't hear what she said, but whatever she told him was enough to get him to crumble.

Michael's shoulders dropped, and he slowly turned away. He wouldn't stop the beating, and apparently, he wasn't brave enough to watch it either.

Madison turned back to Joshua. One nod was all it took. Joshua's fist dove straight into Stanley's temple, knocking

135

him unconscious. He lay there perfectly still. I watched his chest move, waiting for any signs of life.

Joshua's body jerked backward as the school security guards lunged toward him, pulling him away. My eyes went straight to Madison, who stood there satisfied.

"Did you see that?" Zahra asked.

"Yep."

I tried to wrap my mind around what I just witnessed. Madison orchestrated the brutal attack on Stanley, and Michael did absolutely nothing to stop it. Nothing!

As the crowd dispersed, we turned back to our table. I groaned in pain. A sharp pain coursed through my stomach, crumbling my body.

"Girl, are you okay?" Zahra asked.

"Yeah, must have been something I ate."

CHAPTER TWENTY-EIGHT

MICHAEL

"If you stop it, I'll tell everyone your secret."

Madison's words echoed in my mind, building its strength with every second that passed. The threat was enough to paralyze my thoughts. My muscles switched under my skin as my heart pounded with every breath.

"If you stop it, I'll tell everyone your secret."

I stepped back and watched Joshua's fist collide with Stanley's flesh until the cafeteria floor was a crimson hue. I wanted to stop it, but I couldn't. I couldn't!

If anyone found out about the party and the agreement, my world would cease to exist. People would know how I hurt Emma, turning my back on her just to fit in. What

I did was unforgivable. Everything would be ruined. I would be ruined.

Madison knew everything. But how? My heart sunk as the realization came to light. Joshua. Of course, he couldn't keep a secret. Now Madison, and probably Priscilla, knew. They all knew, probably sharing jokes behind my back. I couldn't believe this.

I turned away. The sound of bones cracking, and the thud of Stanley's head when it collided with the ground was too much. The crowd gasped in horror, but I couldn't watch.

I gripped my left wrist with my right, squeezing in hopes of easing the trembling. My breath escaped me. My lungs expanded but wouldn't release. I was choking on my inability to move, to think, to stop it.

I glanced back and nearly collapsed at the sight of Joshua. His eyes birthed fire. Veins pulsated along his arms, leading to fist made of iron. A hint of a smile crossed his lips. He was smiling.

Religion was never my thing, but in a desperate plea, today, I made an exception.

"Please God, please stop this. Please," I mumbled.

Pounding erupted through my ears, but it wasn't the beating of my heart. It was Joshua's fist colliding with Stanley's head, or Stanley's head hitting the ground. I didn't know. Either way, the banging shook my core with its existence. Over and over and over.

My pulse quickened when I spotted the school security guards.

"Yes," I screamed internally.

As the security guards pulled Joshua away, his arms and legs flailed, like a caged animal begging to be set free. Finally, I could take a breath.

The dust settled, and the cafeteria filled with an eerie silence. The coldness of stares blanketed me, but I averted my gaze, staring at my feet. Everyone saw what I did, or what I didn't do. Joshua was an animal for his part in this, but who really was the monster here? I turned to Madison, and her threat emerged from the darkness once again.

"If you stop it, I'll tell everyone your secret."

CHAPTER TWENTY-NINE

EMMA

When lunch was over, Zahra and I said our goodbyes and headed to our classes. On the way, I noticed Amy again, and I couldn't look away for whatever reason.

She climbed up the stairs and disappeared around the corner. I waited a few seconds. Amy reappeared moments later.

Her body had morphed into an unrecognizable display. Her slender body showcased almost every bone. Her light-yellow skin reminded me of a sunny day that began to fade away. Amy's blonde hair matched her skinny arms, thin and almost non-existent. Even her face portrayed a sunken appearance.

When she reached the bottom step, she patted her pockets. Afterward, she turned and ascended the stairs once again. Every day it was the same. As she climbed, I saw another student, captivated by Amy's heartbreaking performance.

The student looked familiar, but I couldn't place her. Maybe I had seen her around the school before. Her eyes followed Amy up the stairs. The girl's shoulders dropped as she hunched over the railing. She sighed, and I could feel her heartbreak.

I shook my head and continued to class.

Later that day, I tilted the pencil as I carefully shaded in the contours of my mom's cheeks. She was the perfect model, still. The pencil replicated her brown eyes, capturing the reflection of the sun buried in her pupils. My mom was beautiful, and against the light, she looked like an angel.

My concentration was partially disturbed by the front door opening. Dad stepped in. It felt like days, maybe weeks since I'd last seen him.

"Hey, Dad," I said, peering down at my sketch.

"Hey, sweetie."

His keys rattled against the side table, followed by his work bag. As he slid off his boots, the smell of sweaty feet filled the room. Sadly, I was used to it by now.

He walked over.

"Another drawing, I see. And what are you..." he began, then sighed.

I glanced up at him and noticed his deflated posture.

"You don't like it?" I asked.

He glanced over at my mom and then back at my sketch.

"What? No, no. I do. I really do; it's just..." He sighed again. "I'm just tired, sweetie."

"Yeah, that's what happens when you work so much, Dad." I sighed, meeting his gaze. Wrinkles now pressed against the corners of his eyes. He looked older somehow. When did that happen?

"You're right," he stuttered. His words seemingly got caught in his throat. "I haven't been the best…"

"Want me to make you some dinner?" I interrupted. "I could make some purple sticky rice. I've been practicing my recipe. No paprika this time."

The recipe didn't include paprika, but I improvised last time, and it did not go well.

He placed his hand on my shoulder. I looked at him and saw redness discoloring his usually beautiful blue eyes.

"Hey, can we…" he began but was cut off by my ringtone, the Minions' rendition of "Jiggle Jiggle."

"Never mind, we can talk later."

"No, it's okay. It's just Zahra," I said, staring at my phone.

"Tell her I said hello." He gave me a warm smile, but I could tell something was hidden behind the gesture.

I nodded and stood.

"County morgue, how may we help you?" I answered in my most professional voice.

Dad's eyebrows drew together, and his lips parted as I stood. I shot him a smile and headed to my room.

"There is something seriously wrong with you," she said.

"Yeah, I have you as a best friend. Oh, and the other billion things wrong with me," I joked.

"Did you see Facebook?"

"Nope, what's going on?" I said.

"Check out Madison's page now, mister!"

"Okay, hold on."

I tapped the phone, turned on the speakerphone, and opened the app. I navigated to her page, MadisonJ4Prez. Her profile picture showed her looking innocent while holding a newborn golden lab. I wondered if Cruella De Vil had the same profile picture.

I scrolled through her posts. One of the first images was of her posing with a few familiar faces—Priscilla, Joshua, and Michael. But Joshua's face was crossed out. I clicked on the comments.

Comment: MadisonJ4Prez: Besties for life! Forty people liked it, with two usernames I recognized. One was Priscilla2Cute, Priscilla, and the other was EMC2, Michael.

Comment: J-Money: Why is my face crossed out?

Comment: MadisonJ4Prez: I'm sorry, who are you again?

Comment: J-Money: What? Are you being serious right now? Shocked emoji.

Comment: PeanutBttrTime (Not sure who that is): Bro, take a hint. As a great prez once said: You're Fired! Donald Trump Meme. Twelve people liked the comment.

Comment: J-Money: Why aren't you answering my calls? WTF.

Comment: MadisonJ4Prez: Sorry, I don't associate with bullies. Toodles for life! #stopbullying #creepervibes

Twenty-eight people, including Priscilla2Cute liked the comment.

Comment: J-Money: Meme of a baby flicking the camera off.

"Holy bonkers, Batman," I said. "I don't get it. Why is she backing away from him now? Everyone saw she was happy about him beating up Stanley."

"People are now saying it happened because of the party thing where she said the n-word. They think it was a race thing," Zahra said through the phone speaker.

"Of course, it was but I still don't get why she would ditch Joshua."

"Well, Tina from math class said her dad found out and blew a gasket. So, Madison…"

"Had to pretend she wasn't involved," I interrupted, finishing her sentence.

"Exactly, hence why Joshua is officially out."

"Oh," I said, finally understanding the severity of the situation.

"Right!? Maybe Madison is finally getting what's coming to her. Ya think?"

"No, this will be like everything else. People will kiss her little Snow White butt, and she'll be even more loved. That's the way the world works," I said.

"Nah, Azizam."

"You know I don't speak freaky-deeky Dutch," I said in my best Goldmember impression from *Austin Powers*.

"Nah means no, and Azizam means..."

"Yo Daddy?"

Her laughter roared through the speakers.

"What the heck was that?"

"Sorry, I was trying to do a yo momma joke but with yo daddy. It didn't work out so well."

More laughter.

"Not at all. Stick to whatever you're good at, chica," Zahra said.

"Can you remind me of what that is again?"

"Well, there's, you know, that one thing...."

"Uh-huh," I said.

"Oh, and that other thing with the popsicle," she continued. "Oh, and how could we forget that best thing of all?"

"Yeah?" I asked.

"Being the world's greatest best friend ever?" Zahra shouted.

"Aww, thanks. That means a lot, coming..." I began.

"Wait, sorry, that title is actually taken by me. Oh, this is embarrassing," she said, muffling her laughter.

"I hate you sometimes, you know that, right?" I said, hoping she didn't hear my smile.

"Love you too, Azizam. Gotta go."

"Bye."

I slid my phone onto the nightstand and strolled into the living room. I paused as the conversation between my parents flowed through the hall.

"I can't do this anymore. I can't do this by myself anymore," Dad said, emotion squeezing every word he spoke.

I heard the sadness and frustration in his voice. My dad was bearing his soul to my mom, and I knew this was a long time coming. They had barely said two words to each other since the accident. It was hard for me to talk to my mom, and I could only imagine what he must be going through, having a partner who no longer wanted to be present.

It only made sense the two would grow apart, and I felt the end of their marriage wasn't too far away. I knew what this meant. Divorce was already written on the walls. And with that came the awkward holiday get-togethers, the constant fighting over who loves who more, and the bitterness in every smile. Love didn't remain after a divorce. Parents lie to you and say, "Oh, we'll make it work," but deep down, we all know the truth. Sometimes a heart couldn't be mended.

"I have to say goodbye."

His words to her stung, interrupting my thoughts. My heart caught. It was rare to hear my dad be so vulnerable. He wasn't very good at expressing his feelings. Don't get me wrong, my dad was an emotional butterfly, but he hid it well, like most men. I assumed it had to do with his upbringing.

My dad, James Christopher Thomas, was born in the lovely farmland of Dubuque, Iowa. He and his sister, Aunt Kia Marie, were the products of a broken home.

And by "broken," I don't mean their parents were separated, but more like their home was broken, filled with broken memories, broken hearts, and, sadly, broken bones.

My dad said that when Grandpa was younger, he wanted to fight for something bigger than himself, so he enlisted in the Army and was sent to Vietnam. Unfortunately, when he came back, he was never the same. His body returned, but a part of his mind remained at war.

Drinking was the only thing to ease the demons in his head. The only problem was that the beer brought about entirely new monsters that preferred violence and destruction over anything else.

And when you no longer have a clear enemy in front of you, you target those around you. My dad took most of the beatings, but he preferred it that way. He would say, "Better me than Mom or Kia."

I once asked my dad why he worked out so much. He would smile, but his eyes vanished to another place. I always thought he started working out to get revenge on the man he called father one day. But it never happened.

Grandpa died on my dad's eighteenth birthday. Dad always said Grandpa just wanted to find one more way to haunt him from the grave, so dying on his birthday was just that. But despite it all, my dad has never raised a hand to me or Mom. I guess even in evil, goodness still blossoms.

My foot hovered as I feared any sound would spook my parents, so I waited for the perfect moment to walk into the room instead.

As I held my breath, waiting, the front door slammed shut. I stepped into the living room to find only the ghosts of my parents present. I sighed and hoped they would be okay. I missed the joy and love they shared. Hopefully, it could blossom once again.

CHAPTER THIRTY
EMMA

"Alright, let's get into our groups. Remember, the project is due in three days," Mr. Greene announced. The class erupted as chairs screeched against the linoleum floor, and students got up to join their partners. I grabbed my notebook from my bag and flipped to my presentation. It was already done, but maybe I could change a few things.

"Oh, and Michael?" Mr. Greene said.

"Yeah?"

"Since your partner is," he paused, trying to figure out the wording, "unavailable, you'll be working with Emma."

I slowly raised my head and stared at the teacher. My jaw dropped as I subconsciously began shaking my head.

I immediately stopped when Michael turned around and peered at me.

"Now we're even. Grab your stuff and sit by your new partner."

My heart skipped a beat as I watched Michael shove his notebook into his bag, smushing papers to the bottom. He walked over, his eyes never leaving mine. When he sat down, I looked forward, as if I were focused on whatever Mr. Greene was discussing.

Somehow, this was all Madison's fault. I didn't know how yet, but I was sure I could come up with at least six reasons if given the chance.

"Hey," a voice from beside me said.

I felt unease, unable to sit still, and a burning sensation flowed through me. I turned to him. He sat leaning forward; his eyes honed on me—the same eyes I would get lost in for hours. But now, all I saw was betrayal, and all I felt was anger.

"What do you think we should do?" he said.

"Huh?" My words seemed to get choked up in my throat.

"For the project. What should we do for the project?"

"Oh," I said. "Uh, well..."

I should have told him my project was already done, a perk of not having a life. In my world, projects got done when they were assigned.

"Well, I was thinking maybe..." I began.

"Let me guess, an organization to help abused animals?" Michael said, cutting me off with a smile.

I shot him a smirk.

"Same old Emma. Always thinking about the animals."

"Whatever. I wasn't going to say abused animals," I huffed. I flipped my journal and began sketching.

"Okay. My bad. Sorry."

Moments later, my pencil froze mid-stroke.

"Fine, I was, but..."

Michael erupted in laughter.

"I knew it. I knew it," he said, covering his curled fist with his mouth. The habit of hiding his smile remained, even though the braces and crooked teeth didn't.

When he lowered his hand, I glanced at his lips but quickly turned away.

"What the hell was that," I scowled myself, going back to my sketch.

"Awh, Em. You…"

"Don't call me that. I'm not Em to you anymore. Understand?" My tone was sharp and direct. I didn't look up, but I saw him nod from the corner of my eye.

"It's just that you always loved animals, and I…" He paused, and we sat in silence for a moment. The only sound in our station was my pencil furiously sketching against the white canvas. The smell of lead floated from the page.

A few seconds later, he began snickering and then shook his head, smiling at a private joke.

"You used to love animals so much; I was convinced Sarah McLachlan gave you PTSD when you were twelve. Remember all those abused animal videos?" Michael said with a slight chuckle.

I couldn't believe he remembered that. I wanted to punch him in the face or hit him with something. Okay, I wasn't violent and couldn't even think of how to hurt someone, but that didn't erase the fact that I wanted him to suffer. I felt guilty at that thought. I had never wished pain on someone else. Of course, Michael had to be the one that changed me.

I wanted to scream and tell him because of him, I didn't know what it felt like to be me anymore. I flinched every time a guy touched me, and sometimes I cried myself to sleep because the moment I closed my eyes, all the same vulnerabilities and fears of that night came rushing back. I still woke up in cold sweats, paralyzed by fear. My soul felt numb, and I had no idea how to change it back.

"Whatever," I said in a subdued tone.

My pencil dangled inches away from the paper. For whatever reason, I couldn't think of what to draw. I squeezed my eyes together and finally exhaled a deep breath. Michael sat next to me, scanning the room. His cheeks blew up, and then he slowly exhaled.

"What were you and Joshua going to write about?" I said, finally breaking the silence.

He ran his hand through his hair, making a pained stare.

"Uh, well..."

"Not one idea?" I asked.

He shook his head.

I shook mine in response.

"Abused animals, then?" Michael shrugged.

I looked at him, staring into his eyes. He shot me a half-smile. I looked at his lips and then turned back to my sketch.

The annoying sound of drumming against the desk first caught my attention. With a sharp glance, he quickly stopped.

"Oh, sorry," he muttered.

Then came the humming, which I responded to with unspoken threats to his life through visual contact. He raised his hands in a defensive posture, then motioned as though he was zipping his lips.

Finally, he slid a pack of gum out from his pocket and popped a piece into his mouth. He gestured for me to take a piece. I declined. Seconds later, a giant pink bubble protruded from his lips.

I could feel my insides boiling as he repeated the action three more times. I set my pencil down, flexing my fingers. When the fourth explosion filled the air with the smell of strawberry-watermelon, I slammed my pencil down and huffed.

"I'm already done with the project."

I slid over the paper I wrote, ensuring I didn't get too close to him.

"If you want to make changes, let me know. If not, I'll just add your name to the paper, and we'll be done," I finished.

"But, but…" he began.

I shot him a glance that hopefully screamed, "I don't care what your opinion is; just agree so we can be done with it." He glanced at me, studying me momentarily, then dropped his head to review the paper.

His words floated to the surface after a few more minutes of silence.

"Thank you."

I didn't respond. Instead, I shot my arm in the air and waited.

"Yes, Emma?" Mr. Greene said.

"May I go to the restroom, please?"

"Of course. Go ahead."

I stood up without a glance at my new partner and headed out the door. When I stepped into the bathroom, the aroma of urine hit me, and I ducked down, checking underneath the stalls to see if I had some privacy. All clear.

I dashed into the third stall and locked it. Sitting on the toilet seat, I closed my eyes and tried to calm my nerves. With every breath, my body trembled.

Breathe.

I had to breathe. Every nerve in my body screamed out, and my heart exploded. I just needed an escape, a moment away from him, from everyone. I never imagined being so close to him would cause me to drown in my own memories and emotions.

The door to the bathroom opened, and footsteps led to the adjoining stall. After the squeaky door shut, my new stall neighbor made their presence felt. I scrunched up my nose and headed back to class. When I arrived, I paused briefly before opening the door to breathe, and then I returned to my seat.

CHAPTER THIRTY-ONE
EMMA

After the last period, Zahra and I left the school and headed towards The Beast. Our movement stopped as we noticed a scene taking shape around the corner.

"This is your fault, Maddie. My parents are about to kick me out of the house. You have to help," Joshua said. "I can't lose anyone else in my life. You know that."

He reached for her arm, but she quickly shrugged him off.

"That was your fault. You shouldn't have beaten him so badly," Madison said.

Joshua's eyes went wild.

"I haven't seen Joshua since the fight," Zahra said.

"Yeah, I heard he was suspended," I said.

"He should have been expelled," another kid beside us said. His lips curled in disdain as his sentiment was echoed by several of his friends.

"What? No, no, you told me to…," he began.

"I did no such thing. Did I say 'yeah, Joshua. Put him in a coma.' Did I? Nope," she said. With a smug look, she leaned toward him and said, "This was all you."

Remember the Incredible Hulk and how Bruce Banner's eyes would change color right before the Hulk roided out? Joshua's eyes didn't change color, but you could see when the monster within him came alive.

His eyes went wild as a guttural roar escaped his lips. With lightning speed, Joshua reached for her neck. His other hand balled into a fist and flew through the air. Madison's eyes grew wide. As his fist was inches away, Michael stepped up, blocking Joshua's hand, making it narrowly miss making contact.

Madison fell backward, cowering on the ground. Joshua leaned toward her, but Michael wrapped himself around him, stopping Joshua's momentum.

"I will kill you, you little…," Joshua roared.

"Stop," Michael said. "Bro, relax. Just stop."

Joshua kept reaching out for her, but Michael kept him at bay.

"Get off of me," he yelled. His eyes burned through Madison as he lurched forward.

"Calm down, man," Michael said.

Joshua's body slowly stopped moving forward, and he seemed to relax. His body went limp as Michael held on. After Joshua's rage seemed to subside, Michael released his grip.

"Hey, stop." the school security guard shouted while running over. "Yall, break that up!"

"This is all your fault," Joshua said, staring at Madison. "It's all your fault." He turned to Michael. "Get away while you still can."

He took one last look at her and ran. Michael reached out to stop him, but Joshua was too fast. As the security guard followed, it became apparent he didn't get his job based on his physical attributes. While the security guard seemed pained by every step, Joshua's form was nearly perfect, extending the distance with every stride. There was no way anyone was catching him.

"Holy crap," Zahra said. "That was crazy."

I stared at Michael as he lifted Madison from the ground, ensuring she was okay. She brushed herself off and grimaced.

"Some people," she said, revealing a slight smile.

I smirked. I couldn't believe she smiled.

"That guy is a monster," Zahra said.

I nodded, but secretly, I didn't think he was the monster.

After the commotion was over and the security guards cleared the scene, Zahra and I returned to her truck and headed home. As we pulled out of the parking lot, I stared into the sky. Dark storm clouds loomed over the school. It was so odd. The rest of the sky was a deep ocean blue, with small pillow-like clouds. I shook it off as Metallica blasted from The Beast.

CHAPTER THIRTY-TWO
MICHAEL

Joyner Lucas's newest song flowed through my headphones when I entered school. My head bobbed to the beat as I stepped up to my locker. I reached for the lock and quickly spun it. Twice to the left, once to the right, and finish with the lucky number twenty-seven.

As I grabbed a few from the locker, a sense of being watched quickly rushed over me. The guys a few feet away stared at me, laughing and pointing. To my left, the same. Something on the front of my locker caught my attention from the corner of my eye.

My heart dropped as I slowly closed my locker and read the giant black Sharpie lettering.

"Rapist."

I froze. My hand slowly raised to my lips.

"No. What? No. No." I stuttered.

I stepped back and quickly glanced around.

"Who did this?" I mumbled. "Who did this?" Now, my words were a roar. "Who the hell did this?" It could have been anyone since Joshua had to open his big mouth. Madison? Priscilla?

Everything inside me froze as thoughts of Emma came to mind. Emma? She had every right, after what I put her through. But she would never. Would she?

I grabbed the ends of my shirt and began wiping, but it didn't work. I immediately poured all the water from my bottle onto it, but still nothing.

"Please. Please," I mumbled. "Please come off, please." But the ink was set. "Dammit."

I leaned against my locker, resting my head against my arms.

"No. No. No. No."

"Son."

I turned, and my heart sank. The principal stood over me with a security guard.

"Can you come with us, please?"

"But I…I didn't," I stuttered, but it was pointless. How could I talk my way out of this? I lowered my head and followed as they led me to the main office.

As we walked, I glanced up occasionally and noticed it wasn't just the students murmuring about me. Even teachers shared inaudible whispers, judging me as if I were a monster.

After sitting outside the office, I was surprised when my mom came storming through the door. She greeted the secretary, who motioned in my direction. My mom thanked the lady with a warm smile, but all warmth dissipated when she looked at me.

"What the hell, Michael?" She whispered through gritted teeth. The vein in her neck pulsed as her cheeks became fiery red.

"Mom, I didn't…."

"Ma'am, glad you could make it. I'm Principal Miller." He extended his hand, and they shook. Her face flipped again to a smile. What a performance.

"Please," he said, motioning inside his office.

After settling in the leather chairs facing his desk, all pleasantries soon vanished as the inquisition began.

"Now, Mrs. Brown, we pride ourselves in having a safe environment for our students, where students are free to get a solid education without fear of being attacked or abused."

He slid her a picture of my locker with the giant font graffiti.

My shoulders dropped. Finally, someone understood this wasn't right. I shouldn't be attacked like this, especially since I did nothing wrong. I glanced over at my mom. Her arms folded, while her top leg flipped up and down over her other leg. The principal continued.

"This goes against our core values. It is an outrage to good discipline and respect."

He turned to me and leaned forward on his desk.

"Michael, do you want to explain why someone would call you a rapist?"

"Maybe it's a mistake. I don't know," I said quietly.

My mind raced with ideas. But all my thoughts, all my crazy ideas led back to one person, Emma. It had to be her. I mean who else would dare call me that?

Mom looked at Principal Miller, and they shared a knowing glance. She adjusted her chair to face me.

"I see," Principal Miller said.

His finger roamed around the picture, and he looked back at me.

"Did you, maybe, harm someone in any way? A joke that went too far, perhaps."

"What?" I said.

"Maybe it was by accident, or you were just in a bad mood. Maybe," he paused, "maybe she deserved it, huh? Anything?"

"But I didn't...." I shook my head, leaning forward and switching between the principal and my mom.

"No sir," I said, "I would never. No."

"Michael, this isn't our first time meeting. Heck, it's not even our fifth time. So, please excuse me if I have problems believing you."

"But I..."

He lifted his hand, silencing me.

"For everyone involved, please just tell us what happened," he finished.

"Michael," my mom began.

I turned to her. Surely, she would believe...

"Please tell me you didn't do this," my mom said, wrinkling her nose. She leaned back, as if trying to create more space between us.

Her words sliced through me. My own mother thought I could do such a thing. My eyes went wild as they flicked between the two adults.

"What? I didn't do this," I said. My voice cracked.

She laced her fingers and brought them to her lips. She closed her eyes and took a deep breath.

"Michael Ethan Brown. I understand life hasn't been easy lately, but if you're lashing out because I'm not a great..."

"Mom, I didn't do this," I interrupted.

She stared into my eyes, studying me like a scientist observing a new creature found in the wild. Her eyes shifted through various stages. First, questioning. How could her son ever do anything like this? Then, her eyes filled with doubt, as obvious thoughts crept into her subconscious. How could her son, whom she once loved, ever be this cruel? There was no way. I clung to that thought as her eyes pierced inside my soul. And finally, my heart melted as her worn eyes settled into pure unadulterated fire.

I shook my head rapidly.

"No, no...but I didn't. I didn't...." My words were interrupted by my mom's actions. It happened so fast, yet so slowly, that I couldn't react in time.

My mom leaned toward me, and her hand was in the air before I could finish my sentence. It collided with my cheek with one swift motion, sending a sharp pain rippling through my face.

I groaned, quivering while covering my face.

Mr. Miller shot to his feet.

"Mrs. Brown!" he shouted, his eyes flashing between her and my battered face. "We do not tolerate abuse of ANY of our students. I don't care if he is your son."

She didn't look away.

"Mrs. Brown! Do I need to call Child Protective Services?"

Her eyes tore through me, trying to figure out where she went wrong. That look. That was the look I dreaded receiving but knew was inevitable. The look that said she no longer saw me as her son.

"Mrs. Brown, please." Principal Miller's words were slow and deliberate.

Instantly, Mom snapped out of her rage and disgust and turned to him.

"Sorry," she raised her hands, "sorry."

"Son, are you alright?" he asked, turning to me.

No, I wasn't alright. My mom hated me. Every student in the school loathed me. No, I was far from alright.

"Yeah," I muttered. The simple act of replying shot spikes through my jaw. But this pain paled in comparison to the look Mom gave me. That look of pure hatred broke me.

Principal Miller cleared his throat and sat back down.

"Now, since this is a school and not a courtroom, I cannot send you to jail or anything of the sort. But the proper authorities will be looking into this matter very seriously. I have reached out to a friend in law enforcement," my eyes shot up, "so don't be alarmed if you get a call from the police. Suppose the truth comes out and we figure out what happened; in that case, you will face more serious repercussions than a simple visit to my office. Do you understand?"

I sat there, mouth gapped open.

"Do you understand?"

"Yes sir," I said between tears. I wiped them away.

"Quit your crying. You shouldn't be the one crying," my mom said.

"Now that this is settled, Mrs. Brown, I will need a minute with Michael, if I may. Then, you can take him home. Taking the rest of the day off may be in his and the school's best interest. I'll get the janitor to see if he can clean up the graffiti."

My mom nodded and stood, but she didn't have the heart to look at me. She just walked out the door.

Principal Miller stood and walked around his big oak desk. He knelt next to me, which surprised me. I'd been in this room countless times, but we had never been this close. Perhaps he was sick of it all, too. Sick of my constant disappointment. "You had such amazing potential," he once told me. I doubt he would still say the same. I braced myself, thinking he'd get his own justice like my mom did.

"Son, I saw what your mom did. That wasn't right. So, let me ask this question, and I need you to be truthful. Do you understand?"

I nodded.

"Do you feel safe at home?" he said. His eyebrows wrinkled as he waited for my reply.

I wanted to laugh at the question. How in the world could I feel safe? Should I tell him my mom was an alcoholic who hated the sight of me because I was the spitting image of the only man she loved, who tragically died in a freak equipment malfunction? All this she made perfectly clear through a very drunken confession three years ago. I'm pretty sure those feelings hadn't gone away.

How the hell could I feel safe when I didn't even like myself most days? How could I? If all you saw was hatred in the eyes of the woman who gave birth to you, then her reflection became your truth. So, no I didn't feel safe. I hadn't felt safe for four years and nine months.

"Yes," I began, while slowly opening my eyes, "I feel safe."

My words burned the second they came out. He stared at me, probably trying to determine if I was telling the truth. He wasn't ready for my truths.

He would put on his nice suit and tie every day, stepping out into the world thinking he was about to make a difference, when, in reality, he didn't care. No one cared for the forgotten. No one cared for the insignificant. Would he care that having bloody noses at school were more common to me than homework? That I hated myself because the taunts of others roared louder in my subconscious than my own inner thoughts. Who cares for those who don't even care about themselves? The answer was simple. No one.

After a moment, he stood up. I could hear his knees cracking as he moved.

"Alright, we'll talk again soon, Michael. You may go."

I stood and walked out the door to my awaiting mom.

CHAPTER THIRTY-THREE
MICHAEL

What was going on in my life? What was happening? My mind spun in a million directions. I had to get away. I couldn't breathe. I went to the one place I felt safe and loved. I went to see Dad.

As I arrived, a family was leaving. Their tears hadn't dried yet as a woman wrapped a child in her arms. The kid looked at me. I wanted to tell him it would be fine, but the reality of it was it wasn't going to be okay.

He would probably be consumed by an internal pain like no other. It would cause him to hate the world, including himself. Every little thing would set him off until, one day, one year, he would finally realize that there was no way to go back to happier times. This was his new reality, and he was stuck with it. From that moment on, nothing would ever be okay.

Dad's gravestone hadn't changed; maybe it was a little more weathered, but the star and anchor were still in prestigious condition. I ran my hand down his engraving.

William Alec Brown. U.S.N. Navy Chief, Navy Pride.

I stared at it as if I was waiting for something to happen.

"I wish you were here."

I sighed, as my mind wandered to the past.

***

"Okay, Michael can you come up, please?" Ms. Clark, my third-grade teacher asked.

"Yes, Ma'am."

I scooted my way past the rows of students and stand next to her.

"Ms. Clark, it's my turn to be line leader," Graham protested.

"We're not going anywhere just yet, Graham."

Graham nodded, pleased he still had the coveted position of line leader.

"Right now, I want to ask Michael a few questions. We just read about Independence Day, and you brought up a great point about the military. Do you remember what that was?"

I rubbed my chin and narrowed my eyebrows.

"Uh, oh yeah. That the military protect us from bad guys and help keep our indebenance," I said.

"Independence," she corrected.

"Right, independence," I repeated.

"And isn't your dad in the military too?"

"He sure is. He's in the Navy. He rides a cruiser which has a lot of missiles and stuff on it. I even saw pictures."

Ms. Clark peered behind me, and her face lit up with a wide grin.

"And when was the last time you saw your dad? Is he still deployed?" she asked.

"Yep, on the USS Vicksburg," I said proudly.

"I'm sorry, Michael, but that's not right."

My eyes grew wide, and I began shaking my head.

"No, he's on the Vicksburg. I remember." I could feel my cheeks get hot. I swore I remembered correctly.

Ms. Clark shook her head and then smiled. She placed her hands on my shoulders and slowly turned me around. My heart melted as I stared past the desks and found my dad standing in the back.

Without a second thought, I ran to him, leaping into his arms and hugging him, anchoring him home. My cheeks were wet with tears as I embraced him. Warmth radiated throughout my body, and my heart drummed to life.

"He's back home, baby boy," my mom said. I hadn't even noticed she was there. But I squeezed even harder at her words.

"I missed you, little man," he said, muffled in my neck.

"I missed you too," I said leaning back. I glanced at Mom whose face was covered with a smile. I wrapped my arm around her, pulling her into us.

Our hug was only interrupted by cheers from the other students and several teachers who snuck in when I was in the front. When he finally put me down, I watched as both my parents wiped away tears, and we embraced as a family once more.

***

The memory quickly faded, and I found myself back in the cemetery, staring down at my dad with blurry vision.

"Remember when you came home from deployment and surprised me at school? I hugged you so tight. And mom," I paused, smiling at the memory, "she couldn't stop smiling."

"She doesn't smile like that anymore. Now, she's just angry. Always angry."

"What should I do, Dad? I feel lost. Alone."

169

"If you were here, you'd say," I paused, trying to remember him, "Be patient with people because sometimes you never know what they're going through." I smiled, then paused.

"But, what about me? When will people care about me? When will they see me?"

I shook my head as I paced along his grave. I felt my throat closing up as my chest tightened.

"When will they see me?"

My movement stopped. I stood there, clenched fist, staring down at my beloved father.

"You left me with her. You left me all alone, and now what am I supposed to do? Huh?"

I leaned forward.

"What am I supposed to do?" I yelled.

I let out this monstrous scream and fell to my knees as the tears began to flow.

CHAPTER THIRTY-FOUR

EMMA

"I thought he was going to get expelled after the locker thing. Heard the cops came and everything," Zahra explained as she turned the Beast down my street.

"Really? Was it that bad?"

"Emma, yeah. Some kids said they called SWAT."

"SWAT? Okay, there's no way that's true. Or the school would have been on lockdown or something."

"That's just what people are saying. Don't shoot the messenger."

The Beast slowly crawled to a stop along the curb. I unbuckled and repositioned myself, so I faced Zahra.

"Hey, Zahra?"

"Yeah?"

"Did you write that on his locker?" I asked in a hushed tone.

Zahra slowly turned to meet my eyes. Her lips puckered and twisted as if she was considering how to answer. Then she turned back.

"Nah, it wasn't me," she said raising the volume on the radio, making Taylor Swift's voice boom through the speakers.

"But I wish it was. He deserved it."

I studied her face briefly and brushed off the idea that Zahra could ever do something like that. Of course, I didn't think Michael could ever do what he did and look what happened there. Maybe I didn't know the people around me as well as I hoped.

After losing most of my hearing from The Beast's aftermarket speakers, I stepped inside the house to find my parents leaning against the table. Surprisingly, my mom turned from her usual view and greeted me with a warm smile and a little wave.

My dad, noticing my arrival, lifted his head and swallowed. I could tell he was nervous about something.

"Hey, Emma, are you heading over to the cemetery? Just checking to see if you wanted to come," he said.

My heart dropped, and my face wrinkled.

"The cemetery? You know I don't do cemeteries," I said. I glanced at my mom, who seemed to be studying my reaction, and then turned back to my dad.

"I know, but I was thinking maybe this one time..."

"They creep me out. If it's cool, I'll just stay here. You guys go ahead," I said, shooting my mom a half smile before focusing on my dad. His eyes met mine, and then he glanced over my shoulder at Mom. He let out a deep sigh.

"Okay, alright. If that's how you feel, that's fine," he said.

There was disappointment in his voice, but I wasn't going. They proceeded to the door, grabbing their keys and belongings. My dad opened the door and paused, allowing my mom to walk through. He stood there momentarily and then glanced over his shoulder, not fully turning around.

"I don't think I can do this without you, Emma. That's it. I don't think..." he paused. "I know I can't do this without you."

I stared at the back of him. Then, my mom slowly slid into view. She stared at me with gentle, pleading eyes.

I didn't think it was that serious, but deep down, my heart shattered. The people I loved more than anything were requesting one simple thing from me. One simple thing. That was it.

"Okay," I mumbled. "I'll go."

Neither of them spoke. Mom proceeded to the car, and Dad tapped the doorframe and walked outside. I quickly grabbed my stuff and followed. My parents were already in the car when I locked the house, so I hopped into the backseat, buckled up, and waited. The car turned on, but we didn't move. I looked up, and my dad's pecan brown eyes glared at me through the rearview mirror.

"Do you mind sitting in the passenger seat today? Just this one time."

I was about to protest, but then I looked at my mom, who turned around to face me. She mouthed the words, "It's okay."

I turned back to my dad's reflection and nodded. My mom and I switched seats, and we took off.

Our bodies bounced around as we zipped through the town. We drove past Zahra's house, but there was no movement inside. As usual, she and her parents were probably sitting in front of the TV. I wished she was here.

I wanted to avoid seeing the town. I didn't want to see everyone else living their lives with smiles on their faces. So, I closed my eyes and shut out the world, embracing the darkness.

Before I knew it, our car came to a stop.

"We're here." my dad's voice was solemn.

I got out of the car and walked alongside my parents. The little hairs on my neck stood up. My breathing grew heavy.

My heart pounded, and every step I took was slowed. On top of that, my knees shook with every step, and my stomach churned. And this is why I didn't do cemeteries.

"Are you ready?" my dad asked.

I took a deep breath and replied, "Yes."

CHAPTER THIRTY-FIVE

EMMA

We stepped onto the stone walkway as oval and square-shaped tombstones greeted us on each side. Soft voices emerged from the depths of the cemetery, and a slight tingling grew within me.

The hairs on my neck stood as goosebumps covered my arms. A trickle of new and fresh emotions ran through my veins, feelings I wasn't expecting. The happiness created a smile, while the fear caused my heart to beat uncontrollably. The heartbreak was the worst. It felt like I was drowning on solid land. That tsunami of emotion ripped through my soul, tearing my heart.

What the heck was going on? Was this normal? Was this why people hated cemeteries? Too many memories rushing in at once? I focused on my breathing and kept my head down. Following my dad's steps, I navigated through the cemetery down the stone brick walkway. When his feet stopped, so did mine. We were there.

I stepped alongside my dad and watched his face. His strong features grew weak. His shoulders slumped. His eyes softened, then closed tightly, as if trying to hold back tears. He held his hand to his mouth, and I saw the subtleness of a tremor. Dad was shaking.

I stood in shock. Even with his huge frame, he somehow looked smaller, vulnerable even. I turned to my mom. There was sadness in her eyes, too, but it was different. She motioned for me to look. I swallowed and turned to see what could bring about such sadness.

"Shoua   Lee-Thomas.   Beloved   daughter, wife, and mom."

I stumbled backward a few steps as my heart sank. I reread the engraving again and then again.

"Shoua   Lee-Thomas.   Beloved   daughter, wife, and mom."

Wait, this wasn't right. Everything within me froze. This wasn't right. My mind raced as I tried to make sense of it all, but it simply didn't make sense. I was with her every day. I felt the warmth of her skin when we embraced, saw the light in her smile, and the love in her words. This wasn't right.

"Mom?"

I turned back to her, but she was replaced by a distant memory.

My side ached in pain as my laughter overwhelmed me. My mom erupted with giggles and snorts as she reached out her hand to my dad. He turned away from the wheel and pressed his hand to hers. Of course, they laughed at my expense, but I didn't mind.

"Millionaire, huh," my dad asked, trying to hide his smile.

"I'm serious. People are becoming rich off the stupidest stuff nowadays. All I need is a good niche," I said.

"Like?" Dad asked.

"I don't know. I do fashion or music…."

"No offense, sweety, but I don't think fashion is your thing."

"James, be nice. There's nothing wrong with the way you dress, Emma."

"Thanks, Mom. At least you believe in me," I said.

"Maybe you can speak Hmong. People are always trying to learn new languages. Nothing wrong with Hmong," my mom insisted as Dad nodded in agreement.

"I barely know Hmong, guys."

"It's not that hard. Npe. Kuv. Koj. If I learned English, you could at least learn your native tongue," Mom said.

"Anyways, when I'm a millionaire, I'll buy you your dream house. I'm talking marble tiled flooring, 20-foot ceilings, dual dishwasher…." I began.

"What's a dual dishwasher?" Dad asked.

"Two dishwashers, Dad."

"Nah, we have you. We're good," he said.

"We don't need all that fancy stuff," my mom interrupted. "But a fireplace in the bedroom would be nice."

"What?" my dad asked, laughing at the thought. "With a bear skin rug?"

"Oh no," she said, "wait, wouldn't those be itchy?"

"Are you really thinking about that, Mom? Like seriously?" I asked.

"Well, you did say anything."

"Okay, note to self, don't let your mom watch HGTV anymore. It's starting to go to her head," Dad said.

We all busted out laughing. Mom stared out the window as we paused through town. Large Victorian houses welcomed us. I stared through the large windows, peering into a future life that could be ours one day. Families gathered at the wooden tables, eating home-cooked meals and sharing their experiences for the day.

I leaned forward and placed my hand on her shoulder.

"See, Mom. Imagine living in one of those houses. It's a long way from the one-bedroom house with Grandma and all your brothers and sisters, right?"

She squeezed my hand as she stared, seeing that magic that existed for others.

"And you'll buy me that house from selling cupcakes?"

"Cupcakes?" Dad questioned. "You can't bake."

Mom elbowed him, trying to hide a laugh.

"Well, yeah, I can't now, but just wait. I'll buy you that house, Mom."

I sat back and looked into the rearview mirror. Dad's eyes reflected back at me. He smiled. We both enjoyed making my mom happy. She never had an easy life, so every smile was treasured for us.

The green of the stoplight flickered through the front window as headlights on the side caught my attention. I looked back at my dad, and my face grew pained as I screamed out, but it was too late. Everything changed before I could take my next breath. Metal on metal boomed from everywhere, as a truck barreled through the intersection, colliding with our vehicle. Our world flicked between darkness and light.

Everything happened in flashes of moments. The car flipped, sending our bodies thrashing. The force launched objects into the air, then back down again. I slammed against the window. Pain sprung throughout my body. Then the veil of darkness fell over me.

As darkness blanketed my world, the soft murmurs of panicked voices merged as sirens slowly grew louder, closer. My eyelids were heavy, and I had to force them open. The world came alive once more.

I was upside down. My arms dangled in the air as my body pressed forward. Blood rushed from my head, throbbing in pain.

I slid my hand over my forehead, returning a bloody mess. I tried to free myself, but the world grew fuzzy until it went black.

"Emma, are you okay? Emma!" my dad yelled.

My eyes slowly opened as I tried to focus. Where was I? What was going on?

"Em!"

"I'm okay," I managed to mumble. "I'm okay."

I didn't know if it was true or if I was just so used to saying, "I'm okay," no matter what.

My dad clutched onto his seat belt, trying to free himself, but to no avail. My mom sat motionless, hanging upside down. Her body gently rocked, while her limbs plunged to the ground. Somehow, she looked like a ballerina caught in midair, waiting for her next breath to land gracefully.

Suddenly, a commanding voice rose from outside the car.

"Just stay still, okay? Do not move."

A large grinding sound emerged as fiery sparks shot from the side of the car. I could feel the car shake with every motion. My eyelids grew heavy, and the darkness consumed me once more.

My eyes slowly opened as the brisk wind kissed my cheek. The scent of metal and burning rubber flooded the air. I pressed up, but gentle hands pressed against me, forcing me down.

"You're okay," a quiet voice said. "Take it easy. Take it easy."

A Latina with long eyelashes and one dimple on her right cheek stood beside me. Her deep-set brown eyes rested on me, while her hands busied themselves, grabbing gauze and other medical equipment.

"Mom. Dad," I muttered.

"Some of my guys are looking at them. It's okay," she said. "I need you to breathe and relax."

"What happened?"

My words were slow and drawn out.

"You were in a car accident. Okay, but you're okay. You're safe. We got you out of the car. We'll wheel you to their ambulance and then to the hospital."

"Car accident? Wait, what? Mom! Dad!" I mumbled, every word and breath striking pain within me.

A wild, animalistic cry rang out from the background. It was my dad. His pain and agony filled the air, sending shock waves coursing through my body.

I pushed my way up. Instantly, the woman's hands pressed against me, sending me back down. But I tried to fight. Every time she pressed me down, I forced my way up. Determination seeped from my pores.

I managed to get up. I leaned forward, but the world spun uncontrollably. I closed my eyes and took in a deep, steady breath.

"Fine," she said, "let me help you. I know you're just going to fight me on this anyway."

The woman shuffled towards me, grabbing my arm and steadying me. I stared into her eyes, and she mouthed, "Breathe."

I took a deep, slow breath and took in the chaotic scene. Car pieces were scattered throughout the street. A man staggered in place as he spoke with two police officers. He cried while his hands flew through the air.

My eyes found my dad with a blood-soaked cloth wrapped around his head. Three policemen held him back as he leaned forward, reaching for something.

I followed his eyes to a stretcher. The peaks and valleys of a white-covered form lay perfectly still. No ebb of the chest. No tremors of the limbs. No sound from the voice. The ballerina awaiting her last breath was no more, never taking her final bow.

My heart sank. Every part of me ached. My knees gave way, and my heart, well, it didn't shatter. It exploded with a thunderous surge that seemed to pierce through my soul.

The lady held me up, but every inch of me yearned to run to my mom and dad. I closed my eyes and found myself back in the cemetery.

My dad grasped me in his arms as the pain set in. I cried into his shoulder while I squeezed into him.

"But I…" I began, but my brain couldn't formulate a coherent sentence.

"I know. Shhh. I know," he said, squeezing harder.

My mind retraced every moment with her since the accident: her silence, the constant staring out the window, my dad saying he couldn't do this alone. Why didn't I see it before? Everything rushed into me like a devastating force, collapsing me into my dad's arms, melting away into pain and heartbreak.

CHAPTER THIRTY-SIX
MICHAEL

The sky was filled with an orangish glow as the sun lay its head on the horizon, casting an angelic hue against the city streets. I watched as people scurried by, oblivious to the young man in front of them, screaming out for pain.

I focused on my shoes as I continued down Main Street. Store lights lit up the street as cars, packed with families racing to get home, zoomed by.

I didn't know what to do or where to go. I definitely didn't want to go home and I…The pounding in my chest interrupted my thoughts as I watched a blonde girl walking out of Kia's Cupcakes. Madison.

"Hey," I yelled out.

Of course, she didn't bother to look my way, so I sprinted to her. I got to her as she reached for her car door.

"Madison," I began, struggling to catch my breath.

She jumped back, startled at my touch.

"Oh, it's you. Thought it was that psycho Josh."

"Joshua," I corrected. "You know what, never mind. How do you know?"

Her eyebrows furrowed as she sent me a puzzled look.

"What the hell are you rambling about?"

She opened her door, sliding the pink box with Kia's Cupcake logo on top into the passenger seat.

"My secret."

Her shoulders shrugged.

"You said if I stopped Joshua from," I leaned in to make sure no one could overhear our conversation, "beating up Stanley, you would tell everyone my secret. That secret. How did you know?"

A smile grin crossed her lips as she rolled her eyes.

"I have no idea what your secret is. Listen, everyone has a secret. Threatening to reveal someone's secret is how you get them to be obedient like little puppies. If you don't know their secret, you pretend you do."

She nodded her head and smiled like it was all a joke.

"Seriously?" Anger engulfed me as I stared into her eyes. "Are you kidding me?"

Her hands flew up, revealing her palms.

"Okay, calm down, sparky. It was only a joke."

Her body tensed, but I could see her slowly moving closer to her car.

"A joke?" My words sounded like a question, but based on her expression, it was heard like a threat. "A joke?" I repeated.

"This was your fault," I mumbled to myself, still piecing everything together. The party. Stanley getting beat up. My locker. Emma. "Everything was your fault," I said slowly as if every word needed its own space to breathe.

"Excuse me?" she said, her eyebrows raised.

184

"I stood there watching Stanley get destroyed because of a joke. This is your…"

My fists reached out for her, but before I could grab her, she jumped in her car, slamming the door in my face. I pounded on the window, but before anything could be done, she peeled off, leaving me standing there, bewildered.

I stared at my fists.

"A joke?"

Molten lava burned within me. My hands squeezed tighter as my breath came in short bursts. I stood by and watched my friend get pummeled into the ground over a freaking joke.

"A joke," I repeated.

That was it. I had it. No more Mr. Nice Guy. No more doing what other people wanted. I was tired of being tired, and I had enough! I swore to myself after today, I was only in it for myself. If no one cared about me, then so be it. We'd see how the world liked meeting the real me for once.

CHAPTER THIRTY-SEVEN
EMMA

When we got home, I was so emotionally drained that I collapsed on the couch. I hadn't truly comprehended my new reality; a world without my mom. She was gone.

In my mind, she was just with me, holding me and smiling her angelic smile. I could still feel her. I could still smell the lotion she always wore and feel the warmth in her hugs.

The thought that I was seeing a ghost saddened me. I looked up to find my dad extending a glass of water in my direction. He motioned for me to take it, and I did.

The cool ice water felt refreshing. I needed it. Dad slumped down next to me. He rested his forearms on his elbows, with his fingers clasped together. He sighed.

"How much of your childhood do you remember?" he asked.

I scrunched my eyebrows.

"All of it, I think."

"What about the ghosts?"

"The ghosts?" I asked. My eyebrows rose.

"Yeah. Or spirits or whatever you want to call them," he said, shrugging.

This was the first time my dad had ever mentioned the word ghost. Unless he was talking about Ghostbusters or something like that on TV, he never brought them up.

He paused, staring at the floor. His eyes sprinted back and forth.

"When you were a kid, we used to think you were crazy."

"Dad," I interrupted.

"We did. You used to see things and people you weren't supposed to see. You were telling us about this woman who would talk to you sometimes. And when you described her," he paused. "It was my mom. You were describing my mom."

I sat up and leaned toward him. He had my full attention.

"You saw Uncle Anthony once down by the swings." He nodded but kept going.

"You would see all these people. But you never met them because they died before you were even born. Uncle Anthony died when he was ten, baby girl."

My mouth dropped.

"What?"

"At first, we thought it was imaginary friends, but then we realized it was far from imaginary." A gentle smile spread across his lips. "We eventually sent you to a therapist."

"A therapist?" I asked.

"They had you talk about what you saw, draw little pictures, but you were like four or five. So, your drawings were pretty bad."

188

"Thanks, Dad," I said sarcastically.

"Anyways, the therapist was pretty useless, saying it was a phase and blah blah blah. We wanted to find a better person for you, but it was just too expensive. We finally just gave up."

"Wow." I sat back.

For a brief moment, I thought about what would have happened if they did. Would I no longer be the way I was? Would the ghosts just disappear? Did I even want that? My mom's gentle smile crept into my mind, which made me smile briefly too.

"So, what did you guys do?" I asked.

He huffed.

"Nothing."

He let out an audible sigh, and I could tell this decision was eating him up inside, as if he had left me down.

"Instead, we just watched you. Made sure we were there for you. If you did something in public, we always had an excuse ready. We allowed it to happen if you did anything at home and were there for you afterward. We didn't know what else we could do."

I wrapped my arm around his back, squeezing him into me.

"But sometimes," he paused, "sometimes, it went bad. Sometimes, we'd find you in your room, curled in a little ball, screaming. You'd scream your name, saying, 'I am Emma Mai Thomas.' Repeating our address. It was as if you had to remember who you were like you weren't you. Over and over again. Every time we saw it...."

His body began to shake. He wiped a tear from his eye, sniffling.

"Every time we saw you like that, it would break our hearts."

"Oh my God," I mumbled. My thoughts flew to the young girl shooting arrows. "Like I wasn't me," I thought.

The tears rolled down my cheeks effortlessly as my memories came rushing back. I remembered the uncontrollable feeling that I didn't belong in this world. I truly believed I didn't belong. I knew there was something, no, someone inside of me. Someone was controlling my every thought. Every emotion. Every movement.

I looked up to find my dad staring at me. The whites in his eyes were soaked in red. His face was riddled with unasked questions.

"I remember," I softly say. "Holy crap, I remember. I remember the panic attacks. I'm Emma Mai Thomas. I am eight years old. I live at 409 Chestnut Street." I recited it as if it were part of me. Like, it was on default in my mind.

We both paused, soaking in the silence. Dad leaned back against the couch as we both stared at absolutely nothing.

"Your mom," he began, "your mom would come running to you. She would wrap you in her arms so tightly. I thought she would break you into two."

He smiled.

"She would join you. 'You are Emma Mai Thomas. You are eight years old. You do live at 409 Chestnut Street. You are my daughter.' That always worked. You are my daughter."

His body shuttered, and his tears roamed across his face, but he didn't wipe them away. He allowed himself to feel the loss of his beautiful wife, my beautiful mother.

I lunged towards him within a breath, squeezing him tightly, letting him know this was not his fault. None of this was his fault.

"I'm so sorry," he mumbled.

"Me too," I said.

We apologized, although we knew neither was truly to blame for me being me.

I closed my eyes, and my memories threw me back to my childhood, laying on the floor of my bedroom, with my mom caressing and comforting me. I remembered her, the smell of her lotion, the feel of her cheek pressed against mine, her tears. I remembered.

CHAPTER THIRTY-EIGHT

MICHAEL

"Where have you been? It's almost 10 o'clock."

My mom stood up, knocking over empty beer bottles at her feet. She took a swig of the bottle in her hand and glared at me.

"I went to see Dad."

She opened her mouth, then slowly shut it. Her eyes moved back to the bottle hanging inches away from her lips.

"He left us a long time ago, boy. It's time you move on."

I stepped forward, hands curled.

"He didn't leave us, Mom. He died," I said. My words carried pain with each syllable. "Yeah, it was a freak, stupid accident, but that's what it was. He didn't leave us."

She lifted the bottle to her lips.

"Whatever. Either way, he's gone, and it's just you," she pointed the bottle in my direction, "and me. What a great pair we make. A woman who can't get a raise and a rapist."

"I didn't rape anyone."

My words fell on deaf ears as she snickered.

"Mmhmm." She turned her attention back to the television.

"Yes, may I buy a vowel, please, Pat? An O," the contestant said. Several dings emerged as the co-host walked over, revealing three Os.

"I didn't rape anyone," I repeated.

"A penny for your thoughts," my mom yelled, waving her hands as if she had just won the game.

"A penny for your thoughts," the contestant screamed into her microphone, followed by the applause of the crowd.

I turned back to my mom. Her eyes were focused on the screen as if I was no longer in the room. So, I turned and headed to my room.

I threw myself onto my bed, face buried into the pillow. I used my hands to press the pillow into my face as I let out a blood-curdling scream. Then another and another. After my throat began to dry and my voice cracked, I sat myself up and let my fist take over.

My fist flew through the air, stabbing the pillow and creating indents that were soon replaced by other craters as the punches continued. After several moments, I stopped, too weak to continue. My arms felt like they weighed a thousand pounds, and an emptiness ravaged inside of me.

I slumped out of the bed and reached for my headphones. With a few swipes to my phone, Spotify opened, blasting Kurt Cobain's "You Know You're Right" into my ear drums. My body flailed throughout the room as I jumped and swung my arms, kicking every lousy thought, emotion, everything out of my head. I felt rage consume me, and for once, I didn't stop it. I let it free into the world, and it felt great.

CHAPTER THIRTY-NINE
EMMA

"Are you sure this is the right place?" my dad asked, looking up at the yoga studio.

He pulled alongside the curb, leaning down and examining the structure. The sign read "Past Whispers Studio" in bold lettering, wrapped around a crescent moon.

"Yeah, Dad, I'm positive."

"Plus, you have our phone numbers, just in case we get kidnapped," Zahra joked from the backseat.

"Not funny, young lady," Dad said, with raised eyebrows.

"We'll be fine. Promise," I said, unbuckling. I leaned over and kissed him on the cheek, the first time I had done it in a long time.

He nodded and watched as we climbed out of the car.

"We aren't really getting kidnapped, right?" Zahra asked.

"We'll see," I replied.

The yoga studio was tucked between a dry cleaner and a local gym at the Fernwood Street Plaza. Most people would likely miss it, but according to a few internet searches, it had great reviews and was what I needed to find more information.

The door chimed as we entered, and the exotic incense mixture splashed against our noses. A handful of women were already scattered around the room. One of the women noticed our arrival and headed toward us. She had really short blonde hair and very toned arms. She placed her palms together and bowed slightly, sending the necklace around her neck jingling with delight.

"Good morning, I'm Miranda. Welcome," she said.

"Hi. I'm Emma, and this is Zahra," I said while Zahra waved.

"Oh, yes, Emma. I saw your registration online. Well, since this is your first time with us, welcome. You're in a safe space. Please make yourself at home."

Why did she need to say we were in a safe space? Was there something we should have worried about? Maybe we rushed into this. I regretted spending little time researching this, but it would have to do for now.

"There are refreshments over there," Miranda said.

She showed us around the yoga studio. There were little cubbies to place our belongings, and the bathrooms were tucked in the back. Then, after grabbing some mats, she showed us where we could set up. Miranda gave us time to get acquainted with the studio as she greeted other people who had just arrived.

"If anyone tries to get me naked, I am out of here," Zahra whispered.

I nudged her with my shoulder while we shared a laugh.

We set up our area and began stretching. We didn't know if we should do that, but it felt right.

I watched as other ladies arrived. In total, there were sixteen women. They varied in every sense of the word. A forty-something-year-old woman, who looked like a librarian, dressed in a long flowing sunflower dress, stood alongside a twenty-year-old adorned in all black. Her makeup matched her clothing.

A thirty-something-year-old wearing a New Edition t-shirt and leggings smiled politely as a fifty-year-old sprawled her yoga mat on the floor. Her long silver hair swept the mat as she stretched. But it was clear Zahra and I were the youngest ones there.

Ding. Ding. Ding.

The room grew quiet as Miranda stood at the front. On the floor sat a medium-sized bowl, still vibrating from the rings.

"Ladies, thank you for joining us today. Blessed be the world," she said, placing her palms together and bowing slightly at her captivated audience.

"Blessed be the world," the ladies chanted back. Zahra and I followed suit.

Miranda began explaining who she was and about the studio and the covenant. She explained that the covenant was a safe space.

"There she goes with the safe space talk," I thought.

"This is a safe space for those who want to embrace the spirit world and become more in tune with their inner being," she said.

Her voice had a mesmerizing effect, soft yet deliberate.

"We welcome those that are new," she gestured to me, Zahra, and a few others. "And we'd also like to welcome witches from the other chapters."

The word "witch" sent shockwaves throughout my body. I could feel Zahra's eyes burrow inside of me. I glanced at her. But as I looked around, I noticed we were the only ones freaked out by the word. It never occurred to me that I might be a witch. I was pretty sure that wasn't on the internet description.

After Miranda finished, she asked that we all briefly introduce ourselves. The librarian-looking woman started.

"Hello. My name is Rose, and I've been coming here for roughly twelve years. When I'm not here practicing, I usually hang out with my husband of twenty-seven years and my black lab, Ebony. Or busy plugging away as an accountant."

Okay, not a librarian. Next was a young woman with long, curly red hair.

"Hi, y'all. I'm Rebecca Marilyn Alexander, but my friends call me Peanut. I once had an allergic reaction to peanuts as a kid. Blew up like a balloon. Whew, you should have seen me. Had to be rushed to the hospital and everything. Anyways, let's just say the name stuck." She let out a big chuckle.

"Anyhow, this is my second time here, and I've learned so much. Glad to be here. Oh, I'm single; well, I'm dating a guy, but I'll probably ditch him after the next date."

The room erupted with giggles.

"Yeah, that's it. Thanks, y'all."

"She's my favorite," Zahra whispered. I nodded.

After a few more ladies went, Miranda gestured to Zahra.

"Hi, I'm Zahra. I'm seventeen years old, and I'm really only here to support my friend, Emma. Thanks."

"Well, welcome, and it means a lot that you're supporting her. A lot of us don't have a supportive person holding us up," Miranda said.

"Ain't that the truth," Peanut added, mixed with a few others agreeing as well.

Miranda glanced over at me. She must have seen the fear in my eyes because she mouthed the words, "It's okay." I took a deep breath and began.

"Hi, I'm Emma Mai Thomas. I'm seventeen and a high school student," I paused. I thought about what Miranda said, "This is a safe space." I exhaled deeply.

"I'm here to figure out what's wrong with me. It scares me sometimes, the things I can do, and," I paused again, "I want to know who I'm meant to be."

I held my head down, but I could feel their eyes on me. My heart raced in my chest, and an emptiness inside me emerged. Zahra reached over, grabbed my hand, and squeezed.

"Welcome, Emma. And I hope we can help you find your purpose. But please know, most of us were in your shoes at one point," Miranda paused.

My body tensed as I allowed her words to sink in. For the past few weeks, I'd felt like I was a unicorn in a world of thoroughbreds. Alone, weird, different. But when I glanced around the room, these beautiful, unique women who were complete strangers to me, welcomed me with opened arms. Despite all my complexities, they looked at me like I was one of them. There was no pity, no intolerance, only acceptance.

I felt weightless as I swam in that moment. For once in my life, I felt a sense of belonging. Like, this was where I belonged. A warmth grew inside of me, one that I didn't expect. I looked back at Miranda, who stood there with a gentle smile that reminded me of my mom.

After the introductions were over, Miranda led us in a few prayers. We all prayed to the North, the South, the East, and the West. Then we prayed for Mother Nature and praised her from the trees that blew to the flowers that blossomed around us. We thanked her for the air we breathed to the rain pouring on our bodies. I was amazed at how much we prayed for something I previously didn't even think of.

We followed the prayers with a couple of exercises to help us release the pressures of everyday life. Miranda instructed us to lie on our mats and close our eyes. She told us to stretch our arms and legs while spreading our fingers and toes.

We closed our eyes and listened to Miranda's calming voice. Our task was to clear our minds from all distractions that held us down in everyday life, from our spouses and children, who needed our constant attention to our jobs that demanded hard focus. Our minds were to be void of thought.

"Imagine you are a bird floating in the air. The wind kisses your feathers, and you soar amongst the clouds. Nothing is holding you back. Nothing is keeping you from flying as you were meant to fly. Feel the wind. Smell the freshness of the air. Be the bird."

My shoulders drooped, and a sense of relaxation took over me. I had never felt so alive before. I imagined soaring through the sky, dancing between the clouds.

Next, we focused on grounding exercises. As Miranda put it, grounding helped us maintain the connection between real life and the spirit world. Without it, we might be stuck in a world, unable to find our way home.

I struggled with this one. It was hard to fully grasp how to ground myself, especially since I had just learned I might be a witch.

"When I ground myself, I allow my emotions to run through my body from my head to my feet, into the ground. I allow Mother Nature to soak in that emotion," Miranda said.

Honestly, it didn't make any sense to me. But grounding might be just what I needed. Hopefully, this would help keep my public displays of crazy at bay.

I peeked my eyes over at Zahra, and she lay perfectly still. Her chest glided up and then back. She looked like she was fully immersed and had mastered the art of grounding. As I watched in awe, the slight sound of snoring rumbled through her lips.

CHAPTER FORTY
EMMA

"You are the worst," I told Zahra after taking a swig from my water bottle.

"What? It was so relaxing. Don't act like you didn't want to go to sleep."

"No. I'm trying to figure out what's wrong with me. If you don't want to be here, then go. I can have my dad...."

"No, I'm sorry. I'll stay. And I'll stay awake. Promise." She held up her hands as if she was swearing allegiance to me. A bit of an overkill, but I took it.

After the break, we gathered back with the rest of the group. We were all ordered to sit on our mats and prepare to begin. Zahra and I, not knowing how to "prepare," just sat down, with one leg over the other, and watched.

The lady to my right pulled incense from her bag and lit it. The aero-descent smell wafted in the air, somewhat burning my nose. It reminded me of my childhood.

When I attended ceremonies with my mom, our family would often burn incense to make the spirits of our ancestors happy. My dad's side of the family would use it at church to ward off demons and the evilness of this world. I guess it made sense for it to be used here as well.

I kept scanning. Other women meticulously placed gems and stones at the head of their mats. One woman had a rabbit's foot on her mat. I was guessing she was a newbie.

Ding ding ding.

"Close your eyes," Miranda ordered. No, not ordered, but guided. "Try to empty your mind and focus on the moment."

I closed my eyes and tried to remove all thoughts from my mind. The sound of humming emerged from the darkness. The other women were channeling themselves, preparing themselves for this journey.

While they focused, random, meaningless thoughts crept into existence: "Did I turn off the shower this morning? Wonder what's for dinner?" As I said, I tried to focus.

"Empty your mind and let the spirits of those around you flow into you," she said. Every word was slowed like they were finding their place within us.

I took a breath, and one by one, my thoughts dissipated from my mind. Miranda's words lowered in volume until all that remained was the darkness of my thoughts.

Ding

Silence roamed through my mind as my breathing relaxed. My body grew weightless, and every inch of me softened.

Ding

Amongst the darkness, a spark emerged. It appeared small initially, but the spark grew in size and intensity with every breath.

Ding

Within seconds, the spark had transformed into a massive beam of blinding energy. I turned away, but it was in my mind. I could not avoid it. The brightness and heat exploded, covering my existence.

Ding

Ding

Ding

My chest heaved up as air escaped my lungs. The studio was replaced by a thick forest with large, mature trees. The smell of nature floated in the air as fire embers dropped from above. The crisp air tickled my skin, while birds scattered overhead.

My lips parted.

"We must fight!"

The voice wasn't my own. Instead, it was intense, powerful, and filled with emotion and intensity, like the spark.

"Fight for our people. Fight for our land!"

My fist flung toward the sky.

"We must fight," the voice boomed from my lips.

A thunderous roar of a crowd soared into existence. I could feel eyes burning my skin. I felt their energy, but I could not see them.

I stared into the forest, my eyes scanning right and then left. My heart pounded with every beat, driving my nerves mad. There. There amongst the trees was a man. No, men. They approached, weapons in tow.

My eyes narrowed. My breathing grew calm, and I reached behind me. My fingers squeezed the slender object, and I raised it, bringing it in front of me. My left arm rose. Then I realized I had a bow in one hand, and now, an arrow in the other.

My body moved automatically, with no thinking needed on my part. It was as if this simple act of arming a bow and arrow was second nature to me.

My elbow slowly pulled behind me, and my eyes aligned with the arrow. With a steady breath, I held the position. The men approached with anger on their faces and hatred in their eyes.

My lips parted once again.

"We fight," I whispered.

And then, the arrow soared through the dense forest, plunging deep into a man's chest, sending blood splattering on the tree behind him.

Ding.

My vision darkened until my eyes shot open, and I was back on my mat. My chest heaved up and down as I tried to catch my breath. My legs, no longer able to support me, crumbled my body to the floor.

Two pairs of hands were immediately on me, catching my fall.

"What happened?" I muttered. My strength was gone.

"Shhh, rest now," Miranda whispered.

My eyes closed once more.

"She's waking up. Miranda, she's waking up." Zahra's voice filled the darkness.

The world slowly came into focus, and I peered down at my hand, which Zahra rubbed as Miranda approached.

"What happened?" I said, trying to kick the cobwebs out of my head.

"Are you okay?" Zahra asked. She hurried over, allowing Miranda to sit directly in front of me.

"Emma, you are..." she paused, "breathtaking, you know that?" She smiled.

"What? Why?" I asked.

"You had the entire room freaking out," Zahra added.

"We've had people overtaken by spirits before, but you are far beyond anything I've ever seen." Miranda smiled, but I saw a bit of fear in her eyes, like whatever I did was cool, but not cool at the same time.

I shook my head.

"What happened?" My voice was still weak.

"Why don't you tell us?" she asked. "What did you see?"

"I felt like I was in a dream, but it felt so real."

I looked at Zahra, whose eyes bore into me.

"I was in the middle of a forest and was some warrior or something."

I continued, "I think I was leading an army or something. I gave a speech about needing to fight and then...."

I stopped myself. It all came back to me. The arrow. The man.

"What?" Zahra asked, noticing my hesitation.

"I shot an arrow at some dude. I think I killed him." I paused, staring at the floor as my mind swam with questions.

"Sweety," Miranda began, gripping my hands, "that wasn't a dream. It was real."

My eyebrows shot up, and she quickly continued.

"But it wasn't your reality. It didn't happen to you. Well, it did sorta."

"What do you mean sorta?" Zahra interrupted.

"Have you ever heard of past life regression?"

I shook my head, and Zahra did the same.

"Basically, it's when people experience moments from their past life. But, usually, it's while under hypnosis or medication or something."

She turned away as if lost in thought.

"Wait, she....but she wasn't hypnotized," Zahra said.

Miranda focused her attention back on me.

"No, she wasn't," she said, straining. "I think you experienced something from your past."

She lifted her hand. "Let me rephrase. I think you experienced something from your previous life. That warrior was once you, and you were once that warrior."

She stopped and examined me as if she was looking for some reaction. I stared blankly. I understood her words, but I didn't comprehend them.

"That warrior was once you, and you were once that warrior." Her words echoed in my mind.

"Is that like some poltergeist stuff? Was she possessed?" Zahra chimed in.

"No. Spirits are beyond intense. Some believe the soul within us comprises the many lives we once lived. Most can't feel or live their past lives, but Emma," she paused, "it may be possible she does."

"Girl, that would explain a lot of the issues you have. Like Joshua's brother," Zahra said.

"Issues?" Miranda asked, wrinkling her eyebrows.

"So, my girl—" Zahra began, but I quickly glared at her. "You know what, never mind."

"No, please tell me. What issues?" Miranda asked.

I swallowed and exhaled a long, steady breath.

"Sometimes I feel emotions…that aren't mine," I said. "I felt like I was trapped inside this one guy's body before he, uh, died."

"I see," Miranda mumbled.

"But we weren't related. So, the guy couldn't be from my past life."

"You possessed powers of a non-relative?" she asked.

"Is the word 'possessed' really the right term to be using right now?" Zahra joked.

I shot her a quick glance and then focused back on Miranda.

"A non-relative," she repeated. Her eyes were unfocused, dodging back and forth, as if retracing a memory of information.

"What is it?" I asked.

"If you're right, which I fully believe you are, you may be more powerful than I expected. I mean, yeah, we have seen people having memories of past lives, but this," she shook her head almost in disbelief, "this is something else. Something, amazing. Your power is unique."

Miranda studied me briefly while Zahra's eyes flipped between Miranda and me.

"I wonder what other things you can do if we tried to control it," Miranda said, but it was more like a spoken thought than a statement.

As I waited for her to continue, my eyes scanned behind her. The women that were once in our circle were watching me. Some shared hushed whispers, while others had fear written on their faces. One even rushed out the door as another tried to protest her departure.

"What's going on?" I motioned behind Miranda.

She peered behind her and sighed.

"Your episode freaked a few folks out. As I said, we don't get many people like you here. Some of these ladies are in it for the show. They like to say they are spiritual, so they come here to impress their yoga buddies. But even the true believers are a little taken aback by you and your power."

"My power?" I said. "More like a nightmare."

"No, ma'am," Miranda began, gripping my hands. "You have a power—a gift. Don't ever forget that, Emma. This is a gift!"

I shrugged, but even a forced smile wouldn't appear.

Eventually, Zahra and I gathered our things, thanked Miranda, and headed out the door. She wanted to work with me, but I only told her I'd consider it. Honestly, the feeling of that warrior was too much, too soon. Her ability to kill with such ease was heart-wrenching. To take another life like that was something I couldn't and didn't want to comprehend. All I wanted to do was discover what was wrong with me and why I had this "gift."

CHAPTER FORTY-ONE
EMMA

"So, how was it?" Dad asked as we hopped in the car.

Neither Zahra nor I spoke at first. Our minds swirled with the new-found information. My dad pulled the car out of the parking lot, and the hustle and bustle of our town came alive once more.

"Why am I like this?" I finally spoke.

He flipped from the street to me. I held my head down. There was a tightness in my chest while I let the car gently rock me with every bump. A long, low sigh escaped my lips.

"Emma, you are exactly who you are supposed to be. You hear me? You are my daughter. My beautiful, sometimes

THE MASKS WE WEAR

hard-headed daughter who lights up the room the second you enter. The one who gives me hope that this crazy world will be okay, because there are generous people like you living in it. Who are you, Emma? You're my daughter. And I'll love you from here to the moon and back, you hear me?"

He reached out his hand and grabbed mine while stealing glances at me.

"There is nothing wrong with you," he continued. "Nothing."

"Dad, I didn't even remember Mom was dead. How does that even happen?"

My body trembled as tears flowed down my cheek.

"Who doesn't remember their mom dead? No one. It doesn't happen," I continued.

"Em," Zahra mumbled.

The car glided to the side of the road. A clicking sound arose as Dad flipped on the emergency lights. He unbuckled and shifted his body toward me.

"I…" he stuttered. "I don't know why you have this… ability. But whatever it is, it's for a reason. Maybe it wasn't time for you to say goodbye to your mom yet. Maybe it's a gift because you get to see her again. You get to spend more time with her."

He paused, seemingly making himself smaller.

"I'd give anything to have one more moment with her."

The car went silent as his words clung to existence. I turned to him. Through my wet eyes, I saw him, not as my dad, but as a man who lost the woman he loved. Here I was, complaining about seeing my mom while he sat there, missing her every moment of the day.

"Dad, I…"

"No, it's okay."

He let out an audible sigh, his chest seemingly releasing all the air in his lungs. He continued.

"I don't know why you have this, but you do, and you have a choice. You can look at it and only see the negative aspects or see the good that could come out of it. There is always good. Always."

I nodded, letting his words sink in. I wiped my nose with my hand and turned back to Zahra. She was leaning back against her seat, arms crossed. She looked up at me, but her gaze faded. Tears formed at the edge of her eyes but did not fall.

"Let's go home, Dad."

He studied me for a second and nodded.

The rest of the car ride was quiet. The radio was on, but it seemed like it was far away. As Dad drove, I leaned against the window, watching the town pass us by.

My dad slowed on the gas at the red light and flipped on the turn signal to head down Main Street. I listened as the clicking sound repeated.

Click click click.

As we waited, a single cloud appeared above us. Then, another. The sky covered itself with purplish-blue clouds that shot streaks of light toward the ground. My head popped up with every clatter from the sky. I slid down the window and stretched out my hand.

The coolness of the air tingled my skin, landing deep within my soul. A lightness emerged within me as I watched the car get lost in the shadow of the sky. I turned to my dad, but when I did, he was gone.

CHAPTER FORTY-TWO
EMMA

Within a blink, my world transformed as an intense pain ripped through my chest. Every inch, every movement magnetized the horrific pain. I couldn't move. The piercing agony muffled my screams while the metallic taste of blood and regret stained my lips.

The clouds had morphed into a thick dark blanket hovering over the sky, casting a surreal view. The air was a blend of smells, from the earthy dirt that served as my bed to the burning of metal. In the distance, fires flashed as moans floated into existence. Cries that were not mine.

An Asian man lay before me, eyes wide open, staring into the abyss. All color drained from his skin. Next to him, a young man slumped against a mound, blood oozing from his chest and arms. Both were no longer with me.

Was that my new fate? Was I waiting until I took my last breath? Maybe death would have been welcomed compared to the infinite pain.

My lips opened, and words forced their way to the surface.

"Survive."

My voice had transformed into a man on the brink of death. There was no power behind his words, just hope.

"Survive," the voice whispered.

Even the simple act of moving my lips shot pain throughout my existence. A simple yet complex thought emerged. If the person I had been died, would I die too? The thought terrified me.

"Survive," he said once more.

Suddenly, the world vanished, and I was back in my dad's car again. My hands patted my body, ensuring everything was where it had been. I forced strained breaths from my lips as my head flickered from the clear sky above to my dad.

"Are you okay?" he asked. By this time, Zahra leaned forward in the back seat to watch me.

My eyes flipped between the two.

"Yeah, I think so. It was another dream or whatever," I mumbled.

My dad glanced over at Zahra, who did the same. They shared a similar expression, an expression of concern.

"Emma?" he said.

"I'm fine. Promise," I said.

I hadn't realized it, but my hands still clung to my chest when I looked down. The pain was unforgettable, yet I tried to push it out of my thoughts. I had to remember that I wasn't that man. I was safe.

A sense of sadness lingered in my mind for whoever that person was. He had seen things no person should ever see, but he survived. At least, I hoped he had.

"What happened?"

Zahra's voice reached me from the back seat. I turned, adjusting my body so I could see them both. My dad nodded, so I explained everything I saw and felt.

When I was done, Dad sat wide-eyed, mouth completely ajar. His skin grew ghostly white as he stared at me, like he was looking past me.

"Are you okay?" Zahra asked, noticing his reaction.

He opened to speak, but then closed it. After several attempts, Zahra and I shared a worried glance. Then, it hit me.

"You know who he is, don't you?"

Zahra looked at me with raised eyebrows.

"Dad, who is it?"

Like a switch being flicked, he came alive once more. His head turned, facing the front window, as his eyes slowly shut.

"He survived," he said barely above a whisper.

"Who is he?"

"My father."

We pulled up to Zahra's driveway. Mama Parviz was outside, sitting on the porch swing. She noticed our car, and her eyebrows merged. Then, her face softened, and her shoulders fell. Her hand went up, and she waved in our direction.

Dad nodded and sent a wave in her direction. Zahra leaned forward and wrapped her arms around my shoulders.

"Bye, chica," she said.

"Thanks for coming today. I really appreciate it."

"Of course. Sorry about the whole snoring thing, but for the record, it was the best cat nap I ever took."

"Absolutely the worst best friend ever," I joked.

"Bye, Mr. Thomas," she said, shaking his shoulder.

"Goodbye, Zahra," he said. He shook his head, but the smile was there.

The door slammed with a thud, and Dad reversed the car. I watched as Zahra approached her mom. Mama Parviz wrapped her in a hug. It took several moments before Zahra returned it.

This had to be hard for her; heck, it had to be hard for both of them.

"How is she doing?" My dad's words broke my thoughts.

"Zahra is good."

"Not Zahra. How is Parviz? I haven't spoken to her and Greg in some time. Everything just…," his words trailed off as if he didn't know how to finish that sentence.

"She has her good days," I said. "And other days, not so good."

"Yeah, I bet," he said. His voice grew softer. "I should call, but it was always them and us, you know?"

By us, he meant him and Mom. When someone in the group was no longer there, sometimes the group didn't function the same. Understandable. I only had to look at our family.

I thought everything was normal with us, except the reality was a stark contrast. I had been living with a ghost and didn't realize that…

"I'm sorry, Dad," I said.

"You have nothing to be sorry about. People grow apart. It's natural, especially with your mom being gone…."

"No, I'm sorry for…," I began, not knowing how to articulate my thoughts. "I was so angry at you and Mom after the accident."

"What?" he said, sliding our car into the parking spot in front of our house. After switching to park, he unbuckled and shifted his body in the seat to look at me better.

"You were mad I caused the accident?" he said, seemingly shrinking his size somehow.

216

My mouth opened, but I couldn't find the words. I shook my head and swallowed.

"No, I know it wasn't your fault. Please, know I know that."

I shifted my body to match his.

"I was pissed because I thought you were giving up on Mom."

"Emma?" He reached out for me, but I pulled back.

"I was so angry that you would let her drift apart. All my life, you were it. The perfect couple who loved each other no matter what and we get in a little accident, and boom, that's all gone?"

"Em."

"No, I know it's dumb, well now I know it's dumb because that's not what really happened, but for months, for months that's how I felt. It felt like," I paused, clutching my chest, hoping the heartbreak was lessening. "It felt like you were ripping my heart out. Not, Mom's, but mine. For months I felt like that. Months!"

As my words and tears intertwined, my body curled as the weight of it all became too much.

"I was mad because I didn't want you to give on me like you did her," I sniffled. "I didn't know she was gone," I said between tears. "I didn't know Mom was gone. I ..."

Before I could speak again, my dad's arms pulled me into him. My body would have crumbled into the car floorboards if it wasn't for him.

I cried, soaking my dad's shirt.

"Hey, hey. You didn't know, sweety. You didn't know," Dad said, blanketing me from my own thoughts. "Shhh. It's okay."

"What is wrong with me? I didn't even know my mom was de...." Something inside of me wouldn't allow me to say the words. It was still too raw, too new.

Instead, my tears flowed, and every emotion within me spilled out. I was angry about losing my mom. I didn't realize she was gone. I was embarrassed by how I had given up on my family when they had never given up on me. I was sad that when my mom was gone, I wasn't there for my dad, who had to carry this impossible load alone. I was all these things and more.

So, yeah, I cried. I bawled into my dad's chest, hoping everything would be better. But I knew all these emotions and tears would never bring her back. It would not erase the last few months. All it would do is open my eyes to the fact that my life, our lives were now on a new trajectory.

But at that moment, between all the tears and the cries for redemption, I knew one thing was clear. From here on out, I would live every day like it was my last. And to be honest, I looked forward to walking this path with my dad. True, Mom was gone, but Dad was still here, and I promised to be the supportive daughter he needed. He deserved that. He deserved it all.

CHAPTER FORTY-THREE

EMMA

After the tears had dried, and the hugs became silence, filled with love, the weekend soon came and went. I once again found myself back to being a normal teenager. Somehow, I liked the idea of that normalcy. I even took cupcakes to Zahra's house, and we had a movie marathon like the old days, Mama Parviz and all. It was a good night. The school was even settling down. I had P.E. without any women staring me down. Maybe it helped that we just played basketball instead of archery, but who knows.

Bang

Bang

I jumped at the sound and jerked backward.

"Oh, sorry, I didn't mean to scare you."

I poked my head out of my locker and stood. My shocked expression went flat.

"Michael?" I said through gritted teeth.

He opened his mouth, then immediately shut it. When he opened it again, he finally spoke.

"Can we talk? Please?" He wrinkled his eyes, and I could read the desperation on his face.

"There's nothing to talk about," I roared, slamming my locker shut. I turned to walk away.

"Please, Emma." His voice grew weak. "Please," he mumbled.

I paused. For a moment, all of our past friendship came back to me. The warmth I felt when I saw him. The stolen touches against his skin as he sat next to me. The secret glances when his mind was preoccupied elsewhere. But then, his face leaned over me in a blurred memory. The feeling of pushing away, resisting. It all came back.

"What?" I said. I crossed my arms and closed my eyes. I refused to look at him and figured we would end it right here, right now.

"I...I know you hate me," Michael stuttered, "but you're all I have left. My mom doesn't...," his voice trailed off.

I opened my eyes and saw him like I really saw him. He looked battered, defeated. Joshua's brother quickly swam into my subconscious.

He lowered his head, and a tear glided across his cheek, making a home on the ground. His body shuttered.

"I have no one else. I'm sorry. I'm really sorry."

He picked his head up, wiping his nose on his jacket sleeve.

"I would never hurt you. You should know that. You know that, right?" He set his brown eyes on me.

I didn't want to feel bad for him. I didn't want to feel pity, but I did. Seeing him like this broke my heart. But he violated everything our friendship stood for.

"I trusted you," I said. I unfolded my arms and stiffened up. "I trusted you more than anyone else in this world. Not Zahra. Not my dad, but you!"

His eyes widened.

"And this is what you did to me? You were my best friend, and you," I paused, trying to find the right words, "you violated me. You broke me."

He shook his head, mouth ajar.

"But, I," he began.

"But nothing. There is nothing you can say that will make me forgive you. All of this," I said, pointing at his graffitied locker, "is what you get. You deserve all of it."

My words were sharp like a dagger, and I hurled them straight into his heart, hoping to damage him as deeply as he damaged me. Despite a brief moment of regret, I shook it away and held fast.

He stared at me. His eyes grew red, his nostrils flared, and his lip quivered. I stared him down and looked at him with nothing but disgust. Our eyes engaged in a non-verbal battle, shooting inaudible jabs and uppercuts in the other's direction.

"Why don't you leave her alone, you freak." I turned to see a kid I knew from science class. Sam, I think. When I turned back to Michael, his fist was already mid-air.

His hand collided with Sam's face, connecting securely on his chin. Sam fell instantly. Blood shot out of his mouth, and his eyes rolled back in his head. His body stiffened as if frozen in the same position as it fell.

Michael was on him without a second thought, raining fist after fist. My heart sank. The rage in his eyes sent shivers coursing throughout my body.

My heart stopped as my breath caught. How did the sweet little boy who would cry on my shoulder on his rooftop, turn into this? Was it the emotional balance beam he continuously had to maneuver at home with his mom? No wait. Was this…My mind stumbled at one grave thought. Was this my fault?

A few guys tried jumping in, but Michael nailed them with a few shots before continuing his destruction of Sam's face. As he raised his fist for another shot, I jumped on his arm, pulling him away. His elbow connected against the side of my face, causing pain to instantly throb from my temple as I flew to the floor.

The world faded between darkness and full color. Voices lowered, overpowered by the intense ringing. My jaw ached with every breath.

Michael turned back, eyes wide open. The shock of hitting me must have spooked him. His eyes went from me to his fist to the horrid faces of people nearby. He shook his head and then looked at Sam.

A young girl standing by the lockers wrenched over at the sight. Even some of the football players watching looked away. This violence was even too much for them. I leaned forward and gasped, when my eyes fell upon Sam.

His body resembled a horrifying masterpiece, with red splashed against every inch of its canvas. His face, once recognizable, was now disfigured. Mounds of bruises already formed on his pale white skin. His red hair was intensified by the crimson river flowing out of his cuts. I recoiled, leaning back against the hot floor and then, my eyes slowly made their way to Michael.

It was as if he didn't know who he was. He straightened, standing over Sam's limp body.

"I'm so sorry," he mumbled.

He backstepped a few feet and took off through the crowd. Teachers shouted for the group to disperse, trying to get to Michael, but there were too many people, and he tended to blend into the crowd.

"Maybe we should take you out of school for a bit. What do you think?" Dad said, pulling out of the school parking lot.

"Dad, I just got back into school. I'm fine."

"Fine? Fine? You call this," he motioned to the knot on my face, "fine?"

I slowly nodded and leaned back, pressing the ice pack on my face.

"And Michael did this to you?" he asked.

"Uh-huh."

"Dang. And this was Michael? The same Michael who can't stare someone in the eyes for too long, Michael?" he said, shaking his head.

I nodded.

"You think you know somebody. Well, wait until I see Michael. Imma…."

"Dad! Don't do anything. Let me handle this," I interrupted.

"Emma, there is no way I'm letting him anywhere near you again," he said.

"Please!"

He glanced in my direction briefly and then returned to the street ahead. He exhaled loudly and shook his head.

"It was like it wasn't him. He was someone else," I said. My voice grew soft as I realized the irony of the situation. How was I the one saying someone else wasn't acting themselves? Funny.

The leather of the steering wheel cover crinkled as Dad tightened his grip.

"Fine. But you had better be careful."

I couldn't tell Dad the truth. For the first time, I feared Michael. But that person who tore into Sam with such ease wasn't Michael. It was something else, some bloodthirsty abomination who thrived on violence.

Nausea crept inside me, and the world suddenly seemed smaller as one thought lingered in my mind. What if Michael unleashed that monster again? But again, I couldn't tell Dad that. Maybe this secret would die with me.

"I will, Dad. I will."

CHAPTER FORTY-FOUR

MICHAEL

I turned. Emma grimaced on the floor as my fist hung in the air. I looked back at the guy. My breath caught at the realization of who it was, Sam. His body lay still, perfectly still.

"Holy shit," a voice said in the crowd. I hadn't noticed the large amount of people surrounding me before. It must have been everyone in school.

"He's a freak," another voice said. "Freaking nightmare."

I scanned the horrid looks on their faces.

"Get out of here!" another student screamed, his cheeks hot with anger.

"Disgusting! You freak. Stop it!" screamed another.

"I ...," I began, but my words wouldn't come out.

I stood up, staring down at his body. I was a monster. Sam was a good person. He never did anything wrong with me. He once helped me up years ago after Joshua, of all people, pushed me into my locker. He was the same kid who invited me to his seventh birthday party, when no one else would. The guy who sat with me after my dad died. We didn't even talk. He just sat there with me so I wouldn't be alone. Oh, God. Sam!

I waited until...there. His chest swayed up and down. He was still alive.

"Hey!"

I looked through the crowd. The school security guard was running up, trying to dodge students waving their camera phones in the air.

I turned back to Emma. I had to apologize; tell her this wasn't me. But everything in me shattered when I looked into her eyes. Her usual gentleness was soaked with a rage I had never seen. The sense of belonging usually rooted within her gaze was no more. She didn't hate me. She loathed me and probably wanted me dead.

I swallowed and ran. I cut through the crowd, pushing and shoving my way. The crowd rumbled, shooting daggers in my face. Everyone, I mean everyone, stared me down. Finally, people saw me, and all they thought was I was a freak, a monster.

Before I knew it, I ran down the sidewalk out of the school. I had no idea where I was going.

CHAPTER FORTY-FIVE
MICHAEL

This wasn't happening. Nothing was going right. My arms swung as my legs drove into the pavement. My chest burned from the pace while tears spat out.

When the pace became too much, I hunched over, arms on my knees, panting. I lifted my head and looked around. I was at the cemetery.

I was unsure if my subconscious drove me here or if it was a supernatural power, but I was here. I walked past gravestone after gravestone until I reached my dad's.

My fingers roamed across the engraving, massaging every nook as if it was brail and I was blind. Maybe if I were blind, I wouldn't see the ugliness of this world. I snickered.

"Dad, I need you," I whimpered. I dropped to my knees. "I have no idea what I'm doing. Everything is going wrong, and I don't know what to do."

My hands covered my head as my tears roamed free. My body curled into a ball as everything I held in exploded to the surface.

"Emma hates me," I sniffled, "Mom hates me." A slow, guttural growl escaped my lips, frustrated with the weight of the world against me.

"I don't want to be here anymore. I want to be with you. Everything was better when you were here."

I looked up, hoping he would be right next to me, reaching out his hand and telling me everything would be okay. But would he? Or would he be embarrassed by me?

He was a military man, sworn to protect against enemies foreign and domestic, and here I was with blood-soaked fists, crying like a little baby as if it was me fighting to take a breath. He wouldn't reach out to me, no, he'd call me a freak, a monster. That was what I was.

No, right now, right here, I was alone in this. I was always alone when I thought about it. Even in crowded rooms, I always felt alone.

My mind twisted and turned through the darkness of my thoughts. Emma should have been the first to notice me. She should have been there for me like I was for her.

My chest heaved up and down, and my tears soon dried.

She should have been by my side every step of the way.

A loud growl escaped my lips as my eyes focused on my hands.

She should have been there for me. She should have loved me.

My heart calmed as the tremors inside of me ceased.

I stared at my hands, noticing every line, every mark. My hands were powerful.

"Did you see what I did to Sam?" I said. "I destroyed him." My words were slow and deliberate.

His body fell so easily, so frail. When I felt his nose break, there was a tiny light shimmering within me. I could feel it. And when the blood splattered across the pavement, oh it was something, something beautiful.

"I destroyed him, and she watched. She watched as my fist plunged into his soul." I curled my hands into balls, squeezing tightly. My knuckles cracked. A smile soon formed on my lips as my eyes narrowed.

"Michael?! Michael Brown?"

I turned to see two police officers slowly approaching.

"Your mom told us where we might find you. Mind if we have a word?" one of the officers said, motioning me to join them.

Of course, my dear mother told them where I would be. She was just like them. All she saw was a monster.

Closing my eyes, I took in a deep breath, devouring my lungs with fresh, crisp air. Exhaling, I slowly opened my eyes, enjoying this moment. This may have been the first time in my life that I could finally breathe and feel alive. I turned back to my dad and knelt. I leaned into him and whispered, "If all they see is a monster, then I'll show them a monster."

CHAPTER FORTY-SIX
EMMA

When we arrived home, I quickly looked at my phone: eight missed texts and three missed calls. I texted Zahra back and let her know I was fine, but the doctor wanted us to take precautions in case there was a concussion. After school, she headed right over.

"Your boy is crazy," she said while stepping inside. She wrapped her arms around me, squeezing the life out of me. "Are you okay? I'm surprised he didn't try to kill you."

"I can't breathe," I mumbled, trying to break her grip.

"Oh, sorry. Sorry. I was freaking out when I heard," Zahra said.

"Yeah," I said. "I've never seen Michael act like that. It was crazy."

Zahra looked me up and down, stopping on the knot on the side of my face.

"Damn, girl."

I jerked my head back as her finger zoomed toward it.

"It's nothing. I'm fine."

"Why are you doing that?" she asked. Her eyebrows pinched as she stared at me.

"Doing what?" I shrugged.

"Doing that. Defending Michael. Still. That dude has put you through hell, and you still stand here acting like he's the sweet little puppy trying to hump your leg."

"Whatever," I said, dodging her and heading to my room. She followed but was far from over from this conversation.

"Seriously. What superpower does he have over you?"

I hopped onto my bed, rolling my eyes.

"Wait. Do you like him?" Her words were filled more with disgust than curiosity. She plopped down in my chair, stretching out her legs.

"Well?" she asked.

"Well, what?"

"Do you like him? Like, like him, like him?" she asked.

I sighed.

"Yes. No. Honestly, I don't know. It's hard to explain. We have been close for as long as I can remember. It's like he is…we are," I stuttered, trying to formulate the right words. "It's like we were meant to be together."

Her eyebrows furrowed as she lifted her chin.

"After the party, I felt lost. Like, if I couldn't trust him, then I couldn't trust anyone."

I stared down at my carpet. A medium-sized brown stain stared back. My feet pressed against the carpet, curling my toes into the fabric. Note to self: never leave your cup of hot cocoa on the floor during sleepover dance parties.

"Gee, thanks," she said. "Good to know you can't trust me." She sat back and folded her arms. Her leg bounced on the other as she tapped her foot in the air.

"It's not like that. I trust you..." I began.

"But?" she said with raised eyebrows.

"But I don't want to place my burdens on you. You have enough on your plate."

She pinched her lips. Her left fingers roamed up her right arm as she stared down at the oval-shaped patterns on her arm. I watched as her chest expanded and deflated, more pronounced than usual.

"Yeah," she finally said.

I sighed. Silence rested between us, and I wasn't sure what to say. Maybe she finally realized why my burdens weren't hers to share. She had done enough for me.

I looked around my room, filled with posters of male celebrities and Wonder Woman. On my desk, there were pictures hung of past memories. Blank spaces remained from the photos I took with Michael and me. There were a lot of empty spaces.

"He looked crazy," Zahra said. I peered over at her and noticed her face buried in her phone.

"Who?"

"Michael," she said. Her eyes reflected the image on her cell screen.

"What are you watching?"

"The video." She glanced at me. "Uh...of the fight."

"There was a video?" I asked.

She stood and nearly ran to me.

"Look."

I watched as her hand glided across her phone, rewinding to the beginning. Michael was pummeling Sam mercifully. With every punch, the sound of miniature thuds boomed through the speakers. Sam's head bounced off the ground as Michael's fist flowed unrhythmically.

My heart dropped as memories of that moment replayed in my mind. I didn't need a video. It was already engraved in my mind on an endless loop, replaying in agonizing detail.

"Watch, this is probably a better angle," she said, flipping to another video. "Wait, sorry. This is the wrong one."

Her thumb flipped between tens of videos of the same event but at different angles, different students serving as their own cameramen.

"Oh, here it is. You can see Sam's head crack on the cement in this one. I almost passed out the first time I watched it," she said, curling her lips.

I turned away, refusing to look. When I tried to swallow, vomit surfaced from within. I couldn't watch it., any of it. I never wanted to watch it again.

I leaned back and scooted to the pillows. My tears ran down the side of my face as Zahra soon joined me. Her shoulder pressed against mine as we both stared at the ceiling.

Silence lingered between us as thoughts of Michael roamed in my head. Then, my mom. Everything in the last few weeks exploded inside my thoughts, sending an emotional hurricane swirling around. I squeezed my eyes shut, trying to kick it all out of my head.

Zahra's hand slipped over mine.

"I'm sorry," she said, finally.

"Me too," I said barely above a whisper.

The night ended with a quiet dinner my dad had made. Nothing fancy, just frozen chicken patties he threw in the air fryer and some one-minute instant rice. Zahra didn't stay.

CHAPTER FORTY-SEVEN
MICHAEL

"You are the luckiest little boy in the world. I can't even look at you. Go to your room," my mother roared.

I closed the front door and stared at her. I never noticed how frail she was. She had always worked out before, but now the only thing she lifted was a beer bottle. I seriously doubted she could defend herself.

"Do you hear me talking to you?" She shot up to my face. "Room. Now!"

I stared at her. Her eyes narrowed as she leaned forward. But for once, I wasn't intimidated anymore. She looked weak to me. I smiled, causing her eyebrows to wrinkle.

"Yes, Mother," I said. A deeper, darker voice emerged from my lips. I guess it spooked both of us because while she looked terrified and shuffled backward, nearly running over the coffee table, I smiled. Finally, my voice matched the real me.

No more timid little boy, easily picked on. No more hiding in the shadows. No more letting my voice be drowned by the world. This was the real me and he wasn't going anywhere.

As she fixed her posture, I watched her. Her body seemed to shrink into itself. Her gaze darted, staring at me. Stepping past her, I scoffed and headed to my room.

I opened my door and looked around. It was pathetic. No wonder why I didn't have any friends. I stepped to my sports posters and ripped them down. Then came the Avenger action figures from my shelf. Everything came down.

I tossed my blue plaid blanket off the bed as well. I stepped to the taped pictures on the wall. Images of Madison, Priscilla, Joshua, and I clung for life as I ripped each one down: the picture of us taking a selfie at a house party, the image of Joshua with his arm around my neck while we smiled at the camera. My fingers grasped the image of the four of us sitting on the bleachers at a school pep rally. When I pulled that one down, the paint from the wall came off.

Each image displayed the same ironic scene: my so-called friends staring into the camera, and there I was, smiling like I was somebody. I snorted, realizing each picture portrayed lies wrapped in more lies. They never cared about me. They used me just like everyone else. And to think, being with them, being loved and accepted was all I ever wanted.

My fingers dangled inches away at an image of Emma and me sitting on the roof, smiling at each other. That was when I noticed it. My smile was different in that picture compared to the rest. My smile was genuine, authentic. I paused. My fingers hovered over the top of the image, contemplating whether this image was worth saving.

Maybe there was still a chance I could fix all of this. Go back to the way things were. Just, me and Emma, on the rooftop, laughing like the rest of the world didn't exist. Just the two of us. My heart grew still, as the brightness of the thought faded, allowing my truth to bubble over.

Emma started all this. She was the one who turned her back on me, when I needed her the most. My veins pulsated as I took a breath and then furiously ripped the image in half, tossing it with the rest of the reminders of the fake friendships and broken promises. I didn't need them. I didn't need anyone.

Later that night, the subtle tapping on the front door woke me. I turned over, staring at my alarm clock: 2:45. I slumped out of bed and let out a big stretch. My body felt heavy, and my eyes fought to stay open. I got to my feet and drudged to the door.

Mom was sprawled on the couch, her head buried in the cushions and her arms stretched out. Three more beer bottles had joined her collection on the floor. I wasn't surprised. I shook my head as the knocking began again.

I leaned in and peered into the peephole. My heart dropped, and a strange tingle floated up my arms. I licked my lips and turned back to my mom. With a deep breath, I opened the door.

"Hey, man."

Seeing him brought memories rushing back, memories I wanted to avoid.

CHAPTER FORTY-EIGHT
MICHAEL
Three months ago

"Hey, Michael. Michael," a voice called out. I turned to see Joshua waving me over. "What did he want? I didn't even think he knew my name."

Emma shrugged.

"Hey, I'll be back. Stay here, okay," I said.

Emma smiled, taking another sip of her drink.

I headed toward Joshua, dodging two guys chest-bumping each other multiple times. Another guy had passed out on the dinner table. On the dinner table. How was that even possible?

Joshua had slipped from the sliding glass doors leading to his back patio. I followed, looking back at Emma as the doors shut.

"What's up," I said.

The fresh night air splashed against my skin as the stars lit the night.

"Hey, I need a favor. You're my last hope, man. Everyone else is so toasted, they're useless."

I looked around at the handful of people sprawled out on the back lawn. He wrapped his arm around my shoulders, bringing me close to him.

"Can you do me a solid?" he asked.

A sudden shiver ripped through my body as a chill breeze rushed through the oak trees.

"Yeah, sure," I said.

"Lifesaver, bro. There are a few more cases of beer in my dad's shed in the back. Mind grabbing them? Maybe five or six. He won't even notice they're gone."

I peered across the backyard. A medium-sized wooden shed sat in the back along the wooden fence.

"Thanks, bro; I gotta run in the car and get the rest of the ice."

"Uh, but," I stuttered.

"Just grab five or six boxes. That should be enough. No more parties at my house. Am I right, my dude? Alright, here's the key."

He flashed a smile with too much teeth and tossed me the keys. They flopped between my fingers, but I eventually got a hold of them.

Smooth, Michael.

The door crept open, revealing various lawn equipment, sports supplies, and a bunch of spiderwebs. I switched my cell phone light on, creating shadows that moved like ghostly figures. My heart raced as I scanned the tiny room.

"Where is the…" I mumbled to myself.

After a few minutes of shifting items and searching over equipment, I came up empty. Maybe Joshua meant another shed. I wandered along the fence, hoping to see another storage unit or something. But I couldn't find anything, no cases of beer and no other shed.

When I went back to the back patio, Joshua was gone. I moved to the front of the house, but he wasn't in his car or the front yard. I figured he must have gotten distracted by a beer pong tournament or a mirror, so I returned to get Emma.

The party music was still bumping as people mashed their bodies against one another. Mustiness floated through the room, drowned only by the excessive odor of the liquor.

My body jerked back and forth as I squeezed by folks dancing. Others expressed their love for one another, interlocking their lips while their hands roamed for other attractions. I glanced away from them after stealing a peak; looked so much different than on TV.

I brushed off my curiosity and kept looking for Emma. She wasn't against the wall where I left her. I whipped my head around, looking through the crowd.

"Emma?" I shouted, only to have my voice drowned by the music.

"Emma. Emma?" I screamed, still barely audible.

I tensed my jaw and stared into the crowd. I pushed through the dancing teens and searched the house. After two laps around the Victorian home, I figured I'd check upstairs.

Everyone knew the upstairs was always off limits, no matter whose house it was. But an ache in the pit of my stomach grew, and my nerves tensed.

I climbed the stairs and looked around.

"Emma," I whispered.

I turned the handle to the room straight off the stairs. But it was locked.

"Em?"

"She's not in here," a female voice replied. Her words were wrapped around sniffles as if she was crying.

"Oh, sorry."

I moved to the next room. It must have been the main bedroom. A large oak bedframe with multiple pillows sat in the middle. Matching dressers and nightstands were positioned along the wall. A huge oil painting hung on the wall, with a couple embracing. It must have been their wedding day. I quickly closed the door and proceeded to the next room.

The door slowly opened, sending the slightest creak floating to the surface. The moon shot rays of light through the blinds, sending parallel beams crashing against the bed.

A dark figure moved from the bed. I stumbled backward. I looked away and began closing the door when a faint voice emerged.

"I love you."

It was Emma.

My posture stiffened. I flicked on the lights as Joshua loomed over her. His tongue traced a sinister path down her neck, while his hands roamed over her spread legs. But her eyes. Her eyes were shut.

This wasn't right. He couldn't do this, not to Emma. What kind of monster would do this? Everything inside of me screamed out as rage surged through my veins, and I lashed forward.

"Hey," I roared. I flew to the bed, pulling Joshua off of her.

"What the hell, man?" he said, collapsing to the floor. "We were just making out," he laughed.

My hand curled into balls. I stood there, glaring into Joshua's eyes. My body shook.

"Relax, skippy. Dang, she's no fun anyways," Joshua smirked.

"Swing," I told myself. "Swing!"

But my body trembled and despite my anger, he was too big, too powerful. Flashbacks of the pain in his punches rushed over me and I simply...I couldn't.

He backed away and walked out of the room. I turned and was by Emma's side within a heartbeat. My hand hovered over her.

"Emma," I whispered gently, not to startle her. "Emma, wake up."

She tossed a bit but didn't wake. She looked like an angel. Although asleep, an innocent smile formed on her face. Her hands served as pillows, and her body curled into a ball like a small child would. She looked so innocent.

A deep heaviness ravaged me, sending my thoughts and emotions colliding. I couldn't protect her, not physically anyway. But I swore I would help her through this, emotionally. Whatever she needed. A shoulder to lean on, check. A friend to calm her when the nightmares overpowered her reality, check. Someone to hold her hand as she told her story, check. I would be there. No matter what, I'd be there because she deserved that.

"What did he do to you?" I whispered.

She was my best friend, and I couldn't survive the idea of something bad happening. Not to Emma!

I leaned in and whispered, "Emma, let's go home."

Her eyes opened slightly as her hand reached up to caress my cheek.

"I love you," she slurred.

Suddenly, the door swung open, and Amy burst through. Her puffy red eyes narrowed on me, as dried tears clung to her blotchy cheeks.

"Get the hell away from her!" She roared. She charged toward us. I put my hands up in defense and jumped off the bed.

"What? But I didn't," I stuttered.

"What are you doing, bro? That's just wrong."

I turned to see Joshua standing in the doorway. His face scrunched in disgust. Was he serious right now?

"No, but it wasn't me; it was…." I started.

"Just stay away. That's not okay. Okay? It's not okay," the girl yelled. She lifted Emma, wrapping her arms around her, steadying her.

I didn't know what to say. I wanted to defend myself, but the anger I saw in the girl's eyes frightened me. Every part of me froze.

The girl shook her head one final time and carried Emm away, gently gliding her down the stairs.

Joshua turned back to me and shrugged. Then, he closed the door behind them, leaving me frozen in the dark. My only company was the silence of the night and my own tears.

When I finally emerged from the room, the party was nothing but an afterthought. Drunken snores replaced the bass of the music and the air reeked of the effects of mixing too much liquor with people who had no thoughts of the following day. Rays of light seeped between the blinds as the sun broke over the horizon, signaling a new day.

My feet tiptoed over the drunken teens sprawled on the stairs and bottom floor. The sound of a shattering bottle, or two, rose from the kitchen. I quickly dashed to the front door, hoping not to be seen. All I wanted to do was go home and pray this was all a bad dream.

I twisted the knob moments away from my escape when a familiar voice shouted out.

"Well, look who it is."

My head swiveled and rage engulfed me. Joshua. My fingers drew together, squeezing into tight, solid fists.

"Come here, man," he said, motioning me into the kitchen.

I paused, caught off guard.

"What?"

"I said come here."

Noticing my reluctance, he motioned to the people scattered around the room, put his finger to his lips, and then curled it once again, motioning to follow.

I scanned the room, then loosened my fists, the outlines of my nails dug into my palms. I swallowed and headed to the kitchen.

When I stepped in, a dozen pizza boxes were piled in the sink. The stools that were once positioned behind the island were now upside down, minus the one thrown through the glass sliding door.

"I know you're mad, bro," Joshua began, raising his hands in defense.

I glared at him, hoping my rage would somehow telepathically strangle him until he cried out for mercy.

"How can I make this right?"

I gaped.

"Nothing. You," I stuttered, trying to find my voice. "You can't make it right. What you did was wrong," I said, hoping my words weren't shaking as much as my body. "You should...," I paused, cursing myself for not remembering all the things I wanted to scream at this guy when I was upstairs.

"$50?" He reached behind his back, pulling out his wallet. His fingers slid through the cash, until his eyebrows began to furrow. "How about $40? I only have 20s."

I stood, trying to find the right words. The nerve of him. My mouth slackened, and my eyes bulged.

"Fine, $60. You drive a hard bargain."

Before I could speak, he stepped toward me, sliding the cash into my hands. Then, he gently patted me on my cheeks and stepped past me.

My soul erupted, and I threw down the money.

"No!" I turned to face him, but he kept walking. "I said no."

His foot dangled mid-step as he slowly turned back to me.

"Fine." He shook his head and sighed. "What do you want?"

His friendly not-so-apologetic expression morphed into a man looking to make a deal. He knew he was caught, and nothing he could say or do could make me turn on Emma.

Ignoring everything inside of me that said run, I stepped to him. I raised my chin, staring into his eyes. Thoughts of Emma pushed me to go beyond my limitations and be strong for her.

"Nothing. You hurt her. Do you not get that? You hurt her." I fought the tears from falling. My throat grew smaller with every swallow, but after a few deep breaths, I stepped past him.

As I rounded the corner, trying to put more distance between us, his words stopped me in my tracks.

"I see the way you look at us. Me, Priscilla, freaking Madison," he scoffed. "I know what you really want, and I could make it happen. How about we make a deal?"

***

My memory quickly faded, and I was brought back to the present. I was back staring at him.

"Hey, Joshua. It's like three in the morning. What the hell are you doing here?"

Joshua was soaking wet. It wasn't raining that hard. He must have been outside for a while. His body shivered a bit as I stared at his bloodshot eyes. I wasn't sure if that was from crying or a lack of sleep; either way, it wasn't a good look.

"Can we talk?" he said. His voice lost all confidence, and he sounded stressed and looked pathetic.

"Can this wait? Like until the actual morning?" I looked back at my mom, but she hadn't moved. I still lowered my voice just in case.

"I heard what happened. That's messed up, man. I'm sorry, bro."

I turned away, rubbing the back of my neck.

"Thanks," I mumbled. "Listen, I should go. Text me tomorrow."

I began to close the door, but he slid his foot in the doorway. When I opened it up, his eyes had changed.

"I know how to make them all pay. All of them."

I stared at him momentarily and then stepped back, allowing him to come in.

CHAPTER FORTY-NINE
EMMA

The following morning, I rolled out of bed and got ready for school. A fresh pot of coffee awaited my arrival in the kitchen, along with a note.

"I'm so grateful for the woman you are. Your mom would be proud of you. Love, Dad."

A warmth grew inside me. For the first time in a long time, I looked forward to what the day would bring. It was as if a weight had been lifted. I felt like I had my dad back. My mind was stable, or as stable as it could be, with the knowledge that I had a— as Zahra would call it — superpower that I couldn't control yet. This marked the beginning of a new me, and I was ready to embrace normal teenager life again.

Maybe Zahra and I would spend the day talking about boys, or the latest K-Pop music video, or whatever normal people talked about. Stepping out the house, I smiled to myself and jumped into the awaiting Beast.

"Hey," Zahra said.

She kept her gaze forward. Her posture seemed hunched as her lips pressed together.

I slid onto the fabric seat next to her and reached my arms around her, nestling my nose in the cuff of her neck.

"You know I love you, right?" I said, still pressed against her skin. "Right?"

A soft giggle floated to my ears.

"Would you get off me? That tickles."

"You mean this?"

I blew my lips against her neck, vibrating my lips against her.

"Girl!"

She pushed me away, curling her shoulder to her ear. But she was smiling. She glanced at me and then turned away.

"I know. I'm pretty lovable," she boasted.

I shot her a smile and nodded.

"And so humble, I see."

"Oh, my humble is all the way up." She raised her hand to the roof of the Beast. "And this is probably the bare minimum."

"Of course," I said.

Our giggles soon died down and we stared out the front window.

"I'm sorry. I know I can trust you. I do. Michael just…"

"I get it, Em. I do. And we're cool."

"We are?" I asked. My smile was uncontrollable.

"Uh…yeah. Was there any question?"

"Well, maybe a little, but just a tad."

She placed her hand over mine.

"Well, now there's not!"

I gripped her hands and squeezed.

"Now, there's not."

After parking the Beast, we entered the school and headed down the East Corridor. I reached for Zahra's arm.

"Hey, wait up a second."

"What's up?"

"I'll be right back."

I made my way to the bottom of the stairs and waited. Zahra peered over, her eyebrows raising as she looked on. Moments later, Amy stepped around the corner and paused, her foot floating over the step as her movement stopped. Her ocean eyes rested on me.

At first, Amy looked away, but my position made it hard for her to avoid me. I stepped up, watching as she fidgeted, and stopped on the step alongside her. She glanced at me and then quickly looked away. The hint of ammonia floated around her.

I leaned in, tilting my head towards Amy's ear. My words were low, and I whispered, so our secrets remained ours. After a few seconds, she gasped and pulled away, never taking her eyes off me. She blinked rapidly as the rest of her body seemed frozen. I straightened myself, gave her a sympathetic grin, and then returned to Zahra.

"What was that all about?" Zahra asked.

"I told her," I paused. "Her sister didn't want Amy to suffer like she did."

"Her sister? Wait, is she..."

"Yeah."

"And you can..."

"Yeah."

"Dang," Zahra said.

As we walked away, I peered back at Amy. She stood at the bottom of the stairs. She stared as if waiting for permission, then turned and walked away.

CHAPTER FIFTY
EMMA

"Azizam," I said in my best Iranian accent.

"That was pretty good," Zahra said, raising her eyebrows and shaking her head.

"I had a good coach. Ready for class?"

"For science? Never. Who cares about the periodic table, anyways?" she said.

I nodded.

She shoved a few books into her locker while I leaned against the wall, staring around us. Two guys from the basketball team practiced dribbling past each other while their friends pointed and laughed. A handful of kids jumped off the half wall, screaming, "Parkour."

A blonde girl I shared English with stood waving a phone in front of a guy. Her arms waved back and forth as her finger went from pointing to him to pointing at the phone. She was not amused.

Suddenly, a sharp pain pierced my chest, folding my body instantly. I reached out, gripping Zahra's wrist, squeezing it, hoping it would relieve some pain.

"Ouch, girl! What the hell…." Zahra shouted. She quickly turned, and the pain on my face must have sent shock waves through her body.

"Oh my God, Emma. Are you okay? What's wrong?"

My body froze as the pain slowly dissipated. Something wasn't right.

"Emma?"

I peered up and met Zahra's eyes.

"We have to go. Now," I commanded.

"Go where?"

Before I could respond, the loud, unmistakable sound of a gun blasted through the hall, echoed by a chorus of screams. Our heads shot up as a mob of students ran from the East corridor entrance.

Zahra turned back to me.

"Run!"

CHAPTER FIFTY-ONE
EMMA

The school erupted in sheer panic as loud thunderous banging boomed through the halls. It sounded like massive fireworks, but I knew what it was. Everyone knew what it was.

I peered down the hall. Students climbed over each other, trying to flee. Behind them was a figure in camouflage, holding a huge gun in his hand. He barreled through the corridor, leaving bodies lying at his feet. Blood had already stained the floor.

My body quickly jerked back. I turned to see Zahra pulling me towards her.

"We have to go!" she shouted. Her voice cracked.

Our legs were in motion before I could grasp what was happening. Students ducked inside classrooms, shutting doors instantly. My body jerked back and forth as we squeezed by other students running in the opposite direction.

More gunfire, but this time from the north corridor. That wasn't possible unless…unless there was more than one shooter. My mind shut off, and all I could think of was to run.

Our feet skidded against the linoleum floor as we rounded the corner. We sprinted down the hall, escaping into the south corridor.

"We have to get out of here," Zahra said through quick, shallow breathing. Her face was flushed and already covered in sweat.

"We have to get out of the school," I said.

I looked around and saw students running for the exit. Bodies climbed over bodies as students ducked for cover. Following lockdown procedures, teachers pulled students inside their classrooms, slamming the doors immediately.

"Oh my God," one screamed out.

"Shooter, shooter," cried another.

"Courtney," the boy, who had been yelled at before, cried as he reached out for his girlfriend, pulling her to her feet.

We dashed down the hall, passing locked classrooms. A panicked voice over the school intercom began to broadcast.

"This is not a drill. I repeat, this is not a drill. There is an active shooter in the east corridor. I repeat…"

The voice paused and then reappeared.

"Oh my God, there are two shooters. There is another shooter in the north corridor. Begin lockdown procedures."

I zoned out the announcement as Zahra and I ran for cover. We had to survive. I refused to have my dad bury another person he loved so soon. Not today, not like this.

"Over there," I said, dragging her with me.

"Crap," a voice called out.

"It's locked. It's locked," said a girl whose body shook with every word.

Our bodies slowed as we looked on. Their faces were painted with sheer panic.

Another stabbing pain ripped within, sending my body folding over. Zahra gripped me, holding me steady.

"We have to move," I shouted. "Everyone, run!"

Zahra and I quickly backtracked our steps as we searched for another escape. One last hallway remained. We turned and awaited our fate.

The hairs on my neck stood as we stepped forward, careful not to make too much noise. Every nerve in my body exploded, and a metallic taste found its way to the back of my throat.

I looked down the hall at the other students, nomads who hadn't found a place to feel safe yet. I recognized one of the others. Madison.

She ran five yards ahead of us, flailing her arms in the air as she reached a door. Banging on it, she peered inside as she snuck glances down the hall.

"Let me in. Please, please. He's coming," she pleaded. "What the hell are you doing? What are you waiting for?"

Madison's confusion quickly morphed into anger. Her body stiffened, and her narrowed eyes bore into the door.

"I thought we were friends. Let me in the door now, or I'll have Daddy fire your father. You hear me? Now! Hello!"

Her fist pounded on the door. Zahra and I reached her side just Priscilla's eyes disappeared behind what looked like stacked classroom chairs. She locked us out. No, she locked Madison out.

Fire burned in Madison's eyes as her cheeks flushed.

"You're done. You hear me? You are done, Priscilla," she roared.

I reached for her, grabbing her elbow.

"Be quiet. We have to…"

"Get your hands off me," she yelled through gritted teeth, pulling her arm away.

"Would you shut the hell up," Zahra whispered. Madison's wide eyes blinked rapidly as she stared at Zahra. I could see the tremble in her body.

Suddenly, the sound of heavy footsteps emerged from around the corner. We froze. My breath escaped me as we waited. A younger freshman I recognized from my art class turned the corner and ran toward us. A sigh of relief escaped my lips.

"Thank God," Madison said as she turned to me. "That was…," she paused. "What's wrong with you? Hello?" she waved her hand in my face as she examined my shocked expression.

When she turned around, she saw the root of my fear. A person in camouflaged military attire stood with a machine gun in his hands.

The person lifted the gun, aligning his light-colored eyes to the sight. The freshman ran straight toward us, blocking our view of the shooter.

A loud eruption boomed through the hall as the freshman was roughly ten yards away. His body arched forward, just to slam back to the ground. The momentum from his run forced his body to slide a few feet before coming to a complete stop. A trail of blood traced his path.

Without another word, we turned, zooming down the hall until we reached the corner.

"Go, go!" Zahra commanded.

The hallway seemed void of life. It sat perfectly still. Classroom doors sat closed to the outside world. The low buzz of the overhead light and our footsteps were the only sounds in existence. We stepped forward, finding one locked door after another.

CHAPTER FIFTY-TWO
EMMA

Zahra, Madison, and I sprinted down the hall, trying random knobs. They rattled but didn't open. We knew the students inside wouldn't open the door for us. How could they know we weren't the shooters? They wouldn't. We were on our own.

"Here," Zahra said, pointing to a class. A younger kid ducked inside moments before we got there.

When we got to the door, it was locked. Zahra pounded on the door. We watched as the student crept inside the storage closet, disappearing from sight.

"We can see you. Let us in," Zahra protested through gritted teeth.

I peered down the hall and saw a shadow stretched along the wall. It approached from around the corner.

I stepped to Zahra and leaned into her.

"We have to go. Now!"

Her fist paused mid-pound and she looked down the hall. She nodded. Madison followed our field of vision.

"Oh shit, shit, shit," she said.

I turned to her, raising my finger to my lips. She nodded and pinched her lips together.

I ran to the class across the hall. A sudden lightness sprang through me as the door opened. My breath escaped me.

"Hey," I shouted in a whisper.

We quickly ducked inside, gently closing the door. Another rapid blast from the gun erupted down the hall, freezing us in our tracks. We looked at each other, sending telepathic messages to hide quickly.

Madison pushed past us and ducked into the far corner of the room behind the counter with test tubes and Bunsen burners perched on top. Zahra opted for a storage closet, while I ducked underneath the teacher's desk, rolling myself in a ball.

My breath sounded like thunder, and my pulse boomed from within as time seemed to slow. Several bangs emerged down the hall. It sounded like someone was trying to break down a door.

Screams rang through the walls, followed by another series of blasts. Then, silence. We held our breaths and listened. Electricity hummed through the overhead fluorescent lights, merging with the squealing tire of a car outside the school, no doubt oblivious to the horrors within.

I squeezed myself tighter. A tingling coursed through my fingertips, and I tried to silence my thoughts.

Footsteps. They approached. Closer. Were they by our door? Were they outside our…Suddenly, the door slowly crept open.

In our rushed thinking, we didn't block the doors. Dang it, we didn't block the doors. I cursed at myself.

Footsteps approached nearly on top of the desk and then paused. I peered down and saw the bottoms of black boots. Blood spray painted the tips, sending my nerves shouting.

I could feel the person waiting for me to make a mistake and come out. Could they hear the pounding of my heartbeat? I held my breath, hoping not to make a sound.

Suddenly, a bumping sound came from the storage closet.

"Zahra," I thought. I peered under the desk again and saw the boots turn and creep towards the closet.

"You can come out. It's safe now," the voice said.

My heart dropped to my stomach as a wave of nausea flooded over me. For a moment, I couldn't breathe. A deep heaviness consumed my insides, and my lungs seemingly forgot how to function. I had forgotten how to live. It was the voice.

I had known that voice for longer than I could remember. It was as familiar to me as breathing itself. But now I sat, confused because that voice shouldn't be here. It should be home, mourning for a loved one. Regretting every misstep, every action, every miscommunication that had come with it. Dammit, I knew that voice. I knew that voice.

The room went silent.

"I said you can come out now."

Still no response.

"Come out here now! You have until the count of five. Five!"

My heart pounded in my chest.

"Four!"

I took a deep breath. My breathing slowed. My mind cleared. Every part of me softened.

"Three!"

I did not fear death. The tingle grew, coursing through my fingers, up my arm, and all over my body. My mind switched to something else, someone else.

"Two!"

I could feel her. I felt the warrior's energy and her spirit within me, reaching out, screaming, "Fight!"

"One!"

Without thinking, I stood up and ran. Before the shooter could turn, I hurled myself on his back, sinking my arm around his neck and wrapping my legs around his waist.

"Get off," he screamed, wiggling to throw me from his back.

But everything in me held on, knowing if I let go, I wouldn't survive this. Neither would Zahra. He backpedaled, slamming my back into the wall.

I let out a painful gasp but didn't let go. My right hand dug underneath the shooter's mask, stabbing his neck with my nails. With one quick motion, I tossed his mask off, revealing a partially concealed face, still covered in a ski mask. His brown eyes, which once felt like home, were now consumed in rage.

"Fight," the voice within me screamed.

He thrashed around again, reaching his arms behind him and gripping my hair. He yanked, shooting lightning bolts of pain straight into my brain.

"Survive," roared another familiar voice within me.

How did we end up here, how did everything go so horribly wrong? My heart dropped at the realization that I was fighting for my life against someone I felt safest around. But despite that I knew one thing was very clear, either he survived, or I did.

With my hand now free, I plunged my right thumb into his eye. He erupted in curses. He leaned forward, pulling my hair again and righting himself. His feet quickly backpedaled again, but this time, he jumped onto the teacher's desk, back first.

His body pinned me to the desk. All I could do was hold him. He thrashed around, knocking over books and a container of school supplies, pens, pencils, and a ruler. There was my opening, scissors.

"Fight!" the warrior yelled.

With my left arm clinging to his neck, my right arm extended, reaching for the pair of metal scissors. My fingers were mere inches away as I stretched as hard as possible. My body lurched forward in pain as his elbow dove into my ribs.

I screamed out, slightly loosening my grip around his neck. His elbow flew through the air again, colliding with my side. Blood spouted out of my mouth as the pain became unbearable.

"Survive!"

His hands latched onto my ankles and slowly pried my feet off him. I feared my fight was done. He leaned forward and quickly collapsed against me, shooting even more pain into my ribs. But this time, he wasn't alone.

Zahra was on top of him, clinging onto his gun, pulling it away.

"Fight!"

I exhaled deeply, wrapping my arms around him again. Zahra bore her eyes into him as she attempted to pull the gun away, but he still had his strength.

I pulled my elbows back, sinking in the choke. The shooter gasped, but still didn't let go of the gun. A blast from the weapon erupted, but neither Zahra nor I stopped.

"Breathe," a voice said.

"Get off me, you stupid —" he screamed but was interrupted by Zahra's elbow.

Another blast. My ears rang, muting the rest of the world. Even with the pounding ringing sound, I still recognized the muffled sounds of a machine gun.

"Fight!"

I pulled tighter.

"Survive!"

I pulled back even tighter, leaning my head up, and then saw it.

"Breathe!"

The chants repeated inside me, louder, stronger.

Another blast, and then, with one steady breath, I plunged the scissors into his neck. Not once, not twice. Three times, four, five. The voices inside of me screamed with every jab.

"Fight!"

"Breathe!"

"Survive!"

I kept stabbing him until his body finally went limp. Blood shot out of his neck as his body crumbled to the floor. I stared at my hand, holding the scissors. My hand shook. Every inch of me shook.

I exerted an exhausted breath and forced myself to sit up. My ribs ached with every movement. My hand immediately clung to my side as I leaned over. My head hung between my knees as blood pooled on the floor.

When I raised my head, I looked at Zahra and stared into her eyes. They stood frozen in time, still as night itself. Her body lay on the floor, blanketed by her blood.

"Zahra," I screamed, ignoring the pain and running to her.

"No. No, no," I screamed, lifting her head onto my lap. I called her name, but she did not respond. There was no pulse. No breath.

The sadness and pain I felt that did not belong to me before failed to compare to the heartbreak I now felt. Everything inside of me caved in. My heart dropped into the abyss as every inch of me cried out for her.

"Zahra. Zahra, no!" I cried.

CHAPTER FIFTY-THREE
EMMA

"I should have done more. I should have stopped him. It should be me, not you, Zahra. Not you. I'm so sorry."

As I clung onto my friend, squeezing my soul into hers, footsteps approached from the hall. I couldn't hide, not with Zahra lying here. I couldn't leave her, not again.

The steps grew louder, closer. My eyes slammed shut as I held her tighter. I took one final breath and waited for the other shooter to come.

"Second shooter down, second shooter down," an authoritative voice yelled out.

My body jerked forward as hands gently pressed against my shoulders.

"You're safe now. Let's get you out of here."

More footsteps approached as the room became a sea of blue and black. Police officers emerged from the hallway, guns in tow, as they walked to the shooter, kicking away his gun.

In the haze of the aftermath, the rest felt more like a dream, like something I watched instead of lived. An officer pulled me away from Zahra's lifeless body, despite my pushing and kicking. But I had no more strength in me. My adrenaline dissipated, and the fighter in me went silent.

The officer led me through the hallway, beyond the carnage. Every step was haunted by echoed screams as sobs caught in my throat. He pressed me into his chest, trying to cover my eyes from the horror, but it was too late. The horror of it all had already sunken into my soul, permanently finding refuge in my heart.

Six. We had passed six lifeless bodies. All six were students, taken from this world before the world even got a chance to know who they really were. Six bodies who all reached out to me, as if I was an anchor to keep them whole. I couldn't. I couldn't save them. I couldn't save Zahra. I couldn't save my mom. I just couldn't.

After what felt like hours later, we finally made it outside. My eyes slammed shut as the world blinded me with its light. I slowly blinked, letting the scene come into focus. A parade of police cars lined against media vans. Snaps from the cameras popped like firecrackers as reporters vied to get their questions asked, only to be held back by a wall of yellow tape.

I glanced across the crowd. Tears flooded the streets as awaiting parents searched for their kids, and students looked for friends. In that moment, I felt every doubt, every heartbreak, every bit of anger. The tidal wave of emotion drowned me, and I floated away into the darkness.

CHAPTER FIFTY-FOUR

EMMA
SIX MONTHS LATER

I sat on the edge of the roof, dangling my feet as my phone buzzed. Pink's "When I Get There" blared from my pocket.

"Hey, Dad."

"Hey. Mind if I work a double tonight?" he said. The sound of a busy hospital filled the background.

"Sure, go for it."

I watched as two small red birds chased one another through branches of trees and between power lines.

"You sure you'll be okay?"

I opened my mouth, then paused.

"Dad, I'm fine. Really. I'm good."

His concern, although usually a tad bit annoying, today was comforting. My mind sunk into the fact that my world had transformed in the last few months in ways I could never have imagined. Dad and I were closer than ever, visiting Mom every few months. I always took her sunflowers, since those were her favorite.

At least once a week, I visited Mama Parviz in the assisted living facility. Mr. Greg had placed her there weeks following the shooting. With the funeral and everything, it was all just too much for her, which is understandable. So, I made sure I visited. She didn't remember me most days, but she had never forgotten Zahra. Oh, Zahra.

My heart swelled as thoughts of her floated within me. I missed her the most. After her funeral, me and her dad spread her ashes into the ocean. She read somewhere that if you get cremated, your ashes will float into space, and you'll always be amongst the stars. I hoped that was right. I really did.

"You go make that money, Pops!"

"Will do." I could hear the smile in his voice. "Okay, see you tomorrow."

"Bye, Dad."

"Hey," he said before hanging up.

"Yeah?"

"I love you, kiddo."

A sweet warmth flowed in my chest. I smiled.

"Love you more!"

I slid the phone into my pocket and then leaned back, enjoying the moment. The night was filled with a beauty that only stemmed from paintings. The clouds hung off the New Moon as mourning doves soared through the open sky.

I closed my eyes and let the autumn breeze brush against my cheeks. Goosebumps spread across my arms, as I took a deep breath. Behind me emerged the sound of feet climbing through the window.

I didn't need to turn around. I knew it was him. Michael lowered himself next to me, matching my posture.

He was always taller than me, so his legs dangled slightly lower than mine.

We sat silently for a moment, staring out at the city. Oakview would be just another blimp in the rearview mirror a few months after graduation. Of course, I would return to visit Dad and maybe the one or two remaining friends.

I turned to Michael, let out a breath, and began.

"I miss you so much, but I'm so pissed at you."

He turned to me, but quickly averted his gaze.

"I'm pissed you thought you couldn't come to me when you needed to talk to someone. I'm pissed you thought you were ever alone. Because I have been with you since day one and I will always…"

His mouth opened, and then quickly shut, allowing me a chance to continue.

"I'm pissed that you weren't there when my mom died. I had to do that without you and that's messed up of you." I stabbed my finger in the air in his direction.

"That was my mom, and you weren't there. And the worst thing, the thing I'm most pissed about is that you treated me like I wasn't worth your time. Like I didn't exist."

I stared into his eyes, so he understood the gravity of my words. No hiding behind fake smiles. No running away. Just pure, unadulterated truth.

"I exist, and I'm strong and capable and worthy of being loved."

I paused.

"I know that now," I finished.

Allowing my breathing to regain normalcy and to quiet my trembling soul, I turned away, focusing back on the horizon.

He didn't speak. Instead, his chin dipped to his chest. A grimace painted on his face. Once I gained control of my breathing, I sighed.

"I'll miss you. The you before things got weird and painful."

His face scrunched and he let out a heavy sigh too, but this time, he didn't look away. His eyes reflected the light of the moon and his skin held this beautiful translucent effect. I continued.

"And I know things didn't end up how they were supposed to," I paused as Zahra floated to my mind. "But, please know I really did love you. You were loved. You really were."

I stared into his eyes, so he understood my truths. His body curled, a pained expression setting on his face.

"But there is no more we. We are done. I need to move on and live my life and I simply can't do so with you."

I paused. The deafening silence was broken up only by the songs from the soaring birds above.

"So, what I'm saying is," I swallowed. "Goodbye."

He didn't bother to look up, so I faced forward and slowly closed my eyes, taking in the freshness of the moment. When the world reappeared, a string of doves soared overhead, dispensing an orchestra of cooing that somehow calmed me.

THE END

YOU ARE NOT ALONE
And if you ever feel like you are then do me a favor.
Close your eyes, take a breath, and then when your world
reappears and you let out that breath, reach out for help.

Dial 988 for the Suicide and Crisis Lifeline.

Dear Reader,

Thank you so much for purchasing and reading this book. I hope you enjoyed it because writing is truly a passion of mine. In fact, I'm always trying to improve my craft and you may be just the person to help me along the way. All you have to do is leave a review wherever you purchased this book. That's it. Your words will not only help other readers discover this story but also shape the path of my writing journey. Wow, and here you thought you were just buying a book to read to waste time, didn't know you were going to make a huge impact on someone's career, did you?

Thanks again for the support.

Signed,
Rodney LaMarr

BIOGRAPHY

Rodney LaMarr's story kicks off in the sun-soaked streets of Lancaster, California, where he embarked on a wild ride of discovery. Fresh out of high school, he dove headfirst into the U.S. Navy, unlocking a world of adventure that would shape his life for over two decades.

Amidst the whirlwind of military life, Rodney stumbled upon two extraordinary treasures. First, he found his partner-in-crime, the love of his life, and together they raised a trio of incredible kids. Second, amidst the chaos of deployments, he unearthed a long-lost love for books, sparking a fire that would soon blaze into a passion for crafting tales of his own.

When Rodney isn't writing gripping novellas or tinkering with graphic design (with varying degrees of success), you'll catch him on the mats, grappling with the art of Brazilian Jiu-Jitsu—where victory isn't always guaranteed, but the thrill of the fight is all that matters.

As the creative force behind the beloved California Dreaming Series, featuring "Miracle's Song," "Miracle's Journey," and "Andre's Story," Rodney LaMarr invites young adult readers on an exhilarating journey of dreams, love, and the courage to chase them against all odds.